HIGH MOUNTAIN CROSSFIRE

Dan Slayter rode toward a patch of timber atop the hill he had used as an observation post the night before. The morning sun was just above the horizon and bathed the steep rock cliffs in thin layers of light yellow and gold.

He was just getting ready to put the radio to his mouth when a shot was fired from the trees. The bullet struck the radio in his hand, shattering it, as a hail of gunfire erupted from the trees. A bullet punctured the left lung of his horse. He managed to grab his rifle and step from the saddle as his horse plunged headfirst into the grass.

Dan knew who had come to get him—and he knew they had a damn good chance of doing just that!

ERNEST HAYCOX
IS THE KING OF THE WEST!

Over twenty-five million copies of Ernest Haycox's rip-roaring western adventures have been sold worldwide! For the very finest in straight-shooting western excitement, look for the Pinnacle brand!

RIDERS WEST (123-1, $2.95)
by Ernest Haycox
Neel St. Cloud's army of professional gunslicks were fixing to turn Dan Bellew's peaceful town into an outlaw strip. With one blazing gun against a hundred, Bellew found himself fighting for his valley's life — and for his own!

MAN IN THE SADDLE (124-X, $2.95)
by Ernest Haycox
The combine drove Owen Merritt from his land, branding him a coward and a killer while forcing him into hiding. But they had made one drastic, fatal mistake: they had forgotten to kill him!

SADDLE AND RIDE (085-5, $2.95)
by Ernest Haycox
Clay Morgan had hated cattleman Ben Herendeen since boyhood. Now, with all of Morgan's friends either riding with Big Ben and his murderous vigilantes or running from them, Clay was fixing to put an end to the lifelong blood feud — one way or the other!

"MOVES STEADILY, RELENTLESSLY FORWARD WITH GRIM POWER."
— THE NEW YORK TIMES

Available wherever paperbacks are sold, or order direct from the Publisher. Send cover price plus 50¢ per copy for mailing and handling to Pinnacle Books, Dept. 2493, 475 Park Avenue South, New York, N.Y. 10016. Residents of New York, New Jersey and Pennsylvania must include sales tax. DO NOT SEND CASH.

MOUNTAIN SHERIFF

SHERIFF

#4: WILD STALLION
EARL MURRAY

ZEBRA BOOKS
KENSINGTON PUBLISHING CORP.

ZEBRA BOOKS

are published by

Kensington Publishing Corp.
475 Park Avenue South
New York, NY 10016

First printing: October, 1988

Printed in the United States of America

ONE

The high rock walls of the canyon rose above the waters of the lake, merging with the deep blue of early morning sky. Behind, the jagged heights of the Bighorn Mountains rose into the clouds.

Sheriff Dan Slayter rubbed the sleep from his eyes and considered leaving the trout alone this morning and just going back to bed. Since coming on the fishing trip three days earlier, he had gotten precious little sleep.

Chuck Farley, close friend and sheriff of Wyoming's Bighorn County, laughed and slapped Dan on the back. It was catch some trout for breakfast, or live for another day on beer pancakes.

Dan agreed that Chuck's beer pancakes needed something to dilute the taste, and agreed to try another morning's luck trolling the deep waters of the canyon lake.

Dan had no sooner gotten into the boat and taken a seat when he heard the low buzzing coming from just behind him. He froze. The rattler, nearly five feet in length, was coiled just a few feet from Dan's back.

Chuck carefully picked up an oar and placed it between Dan and the rattler's head. The rattler's tongue darted in and out of its mouth, sensing the oar, and struck.

The snake's fangs stuck in the oar and Dan moved quickly. Finally the fangs came loose and Chuck Farley then worked to get the oar under the belly of the slithering rattler. Soon the big snake was draped over the oar and Chuck threw it overboard, out into the water.

"That should have woke you up," Chuck commented.

"Too damn big for my taste," Dan remarked.

Chuck nodded. "They grow 'em big in this part of the country. Lucky thing it was the early part of the day." He pointed to the back of the boat, where the snake had appeared. "He likely got some heat from that black tarp lying there."

Chuck lifted the tarp, where another rattler lay coiled. Once again he used his oar, sliding it under the rattler's belly, and then lifting it over the edge of the boat to swim to shore. It slithered through the water with the bigger snake as Dan shook his head.

"Fine bunch of passengers you invite on your fishing trips," Dan remarked.

"This could get to be a disturbing routine," Chuck agreed. "That's the fourth one we've seen in the last two days. And this part of the lake isn't even snake-infested."

"Yes, it is," Dan disagreed. He removed his hat and wiped sweat from his brow, neither knowing nor caring whether the moisture was a result of the snakes or the heat. Probably both. But Chuck Farley had likely saved his life.

For the first time since beginning his job as sheriff of River County, Montana, Dan Slayter was taking two weeks off. Late summer on Bighorn Lake brought the trout and wall-eyed pike back up into shallower water to feed, and brought the rattlers out in droves to sun before the frosts of fall sent them underground.

Dan knew River County wouldn't miss him for a while. He had made his mark as sheriff—the youngest ever to be elected—and was respected by all who knew him. More than once he had gone into dangerous back country to put handcuffs on men who cared little of society and had shot somebody to prove it.

Reared by his grandfather, himself the grandson of a Shoshone woman and a mountain man, Dan knew the trails high in the mountains and how to travel them without being seen. He was known now throughout the West as the lawman who got the job done.

Dan didn't want to think of work for a while. He let his line sink deep into the water to begin another day's fishing, letting the snakes crawl into the back of his mind. But it wasn't easy: the sound of buzzing close by and the sight of a coiled serpent weren't things you just dismissed at random.

Chuck Farley, on the other hand, found it amusing, though he could see Dan's nerves had been strained a little. He was the opposite in appearance from Dan: short and blond, while Dan was tall and dark. Both men were lean and born to the rugged back country of the mountains. And both had logged their share of hours tracking men along high trails. Snakes were a part of the routine, but something you were never really ready for.

"You're shaking your pole a little, Dan," he teased. "Aren't you afraid the fish will notice?"

Dan tried to laugh. "It wasn't your butt that was right next to that rattler," he pointed out.

"You've got to get used to that up in these canyons," Chuck said. "Lot's of 'em here. That's why we don't have no mice." He laughed again.

Dan had gotten to know Chuck very well in college. They had taken some of the same undergraduate courses in plant identification and soil taxonomy. Dan's major had been in wildlife management and Chuck had been getting a degree in rangeland science. They had shared several nights together around kegs along various mountain rivers and had even been after the same girl.

Her name was Mindy. She was always a topic of discussion whenever Dan ran into Chuck at a law enforcement school, or when they got together to hunt or fish. They had both liked Mindy and had had a few arguments over her. But in the end, neither of them had succeeded in getting her.

Instead, they had both been told goodbye by Mindy on the same day—together, at the same place. It seemed Mindy had fallen for a shoe salesman she had met way down the Yellowstone in the small town of Laurel, after spending the afternoon drinking in a place called the Board of

8

Trade Bar. He had given the bar owners a good deal on ballet slippers and had talked Mindy into selling hiking boots with him in Yellowstone Park.

Mindy and her shoe salesman had bumped into Dan and Chuck fishing the Firehole River. She informed them that she was off to a better world with the man of her dreams. Dan and Chuck had drunk to her health, hoping the smell of foot powder stayed with her forever.

After discussing Mindy again for a time, Dan's nerves began to settle down. As the morning wore on, they hauled in some big fish and discussed old times again. When a slight breeze came across the water from the east, Chuck suggested that they head for shore.

"Big thunderstorms come up here in a minute," Chuck explained. "I've had the boat swamped a number of times."

They were nearing the shore where they had made camp, when Chuck pointed to a herd of wild horses that had moved up to the edge of a high cliff. Their leader was a big black stallion, looking down over the cliff and across the water at Dan and Chuck.

"That's the horse I was telling you about the other day," Chuck said, as they watched the herd. "That's a good stallion, that one. He should put some real blood into the wild horse herd up here."

Dan nodded. He hadn't seen a horse with that kind of pride in a long time. He could remember a horse his grandfather had caught for him in the mountains of the upper Musselshell—a big bay stallion with a white blaze down his nose—that had been just about the best horse you could find. Dan could see this stallion was of the same kind of stock.

As they unloaded their gear onto shore, Dan and Chuck watched the stallion and the herd. Dan commented that he would like to get a closer look at the horse, and Chuck told him he knew a road that would take them back into the canyon country, where the wild horse range was.

They were discussing this when Dan noticed that the stallion had become alarmed. The big black tossed his head and led his mares in a dead run along the top of the cliff, his mane and tail flying in the wind.

"What do you figure spooked them?" Chuck wondered aloud.

Dan pointed to a group of riders that had appeared on the skyline, running their horses along the edge of the cliff behind the wild stallion and his herd.

"Horse hunters, it looks like to me," Dan said.

"Damn!" Chuck slapped the side of his leg. "I'd been told about them. But I didn't think anyone would have guts enough to do that on a preserve."

"It looks to me like they're intent on getting that stallion," Dan observed. "Illegal or not, they mean business."

"Well, it's my business to stop them," Chuck said emphatically. "This is BLM land, but the detective is busy in Montana this week."

"Let's go," Dan said.

They left their fish on a string in the water, got

10

into Chuck's old Willy's Jeep, and climbed up onto the rims of rock above the lake. The stallion was by now in the distance, taking his herd into the higher canyon country, where the juniper blended together to create illusions and provide hiding.

The horse hunters were not far behind, leaving a trail of dust that formed a film of brown against the summer sky.

"Whoever's leading the horse hunters sure knows the country," Chuck remarked. "Or they couldn't stick with that herd this long. I have an idea who it is."

Chuck knew the country well himself and decided to take a road that would lead around the edge of the canyon and swing up into the higher country.

"My guess is, that stallion is going to lead them in a circle," Chuck explained to Dan. "We should get up on top about the time the herd comes around the other end of the canyon. Maybe the horse hunters will just run into us up there. I'd like to ask them some questions."

The Jeep bounced up the rocky road toward the open tableland at the summit. On occasion, Chuck would stop and he and Dan would glass the surrounding country for signs of the horses and the horse hunters. The hanging dust was easy to spot and Dan had a good idea where the herd was headed—right where Chuck had predicted.

The Jeep lurched the last rough hundred yards to where the road broke out on top. The soil was thin and the scrub timber was interspersed with stands of sagebrush and tall-growing rabbitbrush shrubs.

Chuck parked the Jeep and he and Dan got out. They both leaned over the hood and trained their field glasses down the ridge, to where the black stallion was just coming into view.

The herd rushed across the top, veering off their main course at seeing Dan and Chuck standing near the Jeep. The black stallion led them in a wide circle around Dan and Chuck, and down into a steep canyon on the other side of the mountain.

"They've been run hard," Dan observed.

"Time to put a stop to it," Chuck said, nodding. "And here they come." Chuck was pointing across the flat to the horse hunters.

Dan could see that the riders had no intention of slowing down, but were intent on following the herd down into the canyon. Dan levered a round into his rifle and ran out into the sagebrush between the retreating wild herd and the on-coming horse hunters.

The horse hunters started to turn off and go around. But seeing the wild stallion and his herd were now getting away from them, they stopped and looked over to where Chuck came out to join Dan.

"There's someone who thinks he owns the world," Dan commented, observing the leader's attitude.

"Nolan Steadman," Chuck said to Dan. "I should have known."

"Who's he?"

"He's a stock supplier for the rodeos," Chuck

answered. "He has a scrub place where he raises mean bull calves for bull riding, but he makes most of his money selling bucking horses. And this is where he gets them."

"How long has he been doing this?" Dan asked.

"It's hard to say," Chuck replied. "The Bureau of Land Management has been fixing cut fences for some time. They tell me they aren't sure who is doing it. It seems to me that mystery has now been solved."

Dan nodded in agreement. He could see from the looks of this bunch of horse hunters that they were all from a line of hardcases, and that they didn't like seeing anyone else in their domain. There was little doubt in Dan's mind as he watched them that there would be trouble.

TWO

The horse hunters rode over, led by Nolan Steadman, and Dan studied the man as he reined in with his gang behind him. There were five dusty riders in all, and it was plain Steadman was in charge. He was thin and wiry, with a week's growth of beard and dark features to make his face look even blacker.

He removed his hat and knocked dust from his soiled cotton shirt and jeans. He was glaring at Dan.

"What do you think you're doing, running out between us and those horses like that?" he asked.

"The way I hear it, you've got no business chasing that herd," Dan told him.

"This ain't preserve land here."

"Steadman, we saw you chasing them up above the lake," Chuck put in. "That's preserve down there. You're out of bounds and you know it."

"That's not a matter for you down there," Steadman challenged. "That's government land."

"You're not on government land now," Chuck told him.

"Like I said, it ain't no preserve, either," Steadman hissed through clenched teeth, pointing with his finger to the ground. "We've got every right to hunt them *here*. And you're trespassing."

"You don't have any right to hunt wild horses anywhere," Dan told Steadman flatly. "It's likely that those horses are marked with lip or ear tattoos. How did you ever think you could get away with keeping those horses? The BLM would surely come looking for them sooner or later."

"Just who in the hell do you think you are?" Steadman growled at Dan. "You ain't even from this country and you come up here to tell me what's what."

"It looks like you need to be told what's what," Dan pointed out.

"This here's private land," Steadman said again. "I can be here and do what I want here."

"But it's not your land, Steadman," Chuck reminded him. "This pasture belongs to Gus and Sadie Wilkens."

"You just ask Gus and Sadie if they care what we do on their land," Steadman said. "You just ask."

"That's not the point," Chuck insisted. "Somehow those horses got from the preserve, where they should be, up here on this mountain, where they shouldn't be. And you're to blame."

"You can't prove that," Steadman said.

"We watched you and your men chasing them," Dan said. "We watched you all the way. Do you think we were waiting here by accident?"

Steadman glared at Dan again. "You didn't see us take no horses off that preserve," he finally said.

16

"Is there a fence cut down below?" Chuck asked. "That's been a problem, I've been told."

"We don't know nothin' about no cut fence," one of the others put in, a man tall and light-featured, with a slice of ear missing on his left side.

"Let me do the talking, Keith," Steadman said. "When I need your help, I'll ask." He turned back to Chuck and Dan. "Like I said, we can be on this land, here, anytime we want. Gus and Sadie wouldn't want you two up here, though. We ain't broke no laws up here and you've got no right chasing those horses off like you did."

"You don't take horses off that preserve just anytime you want," Chuck warned. "Otherwise, you've got trouble."

Steadman glared at Chuck. The men behind him, especially the one named Keith, were getting anxious. They knew they had all been studied closely by Dan and Chuck and would likely be in trouble when the two lawmen got down below.

Dan had been watching all the men with Steadman. He had no idea who the other men were, with the exception of the one Steadman had called Keith. Dan knew he was Keith Larson, an ex-rodeo raider with a long record of run-ins with the law.

Dan had seen Larson's face on wanted posters more than once, as Larson had helped steal cattle from a rancher in the county next to his up in Montana. He had served four years in Deer Lodge for it, but it didn't seem to have changed his ways.

Larson kept eyeing Dan and whispering to the others. Finally, he spoke up again.

"Like Nolan said, you ain't from this country," he told Dan. "Don't you think you ought to go back where you come from?"

"You might end up going back where you came from," Dan retorted.

"Don't count on it, lawman," Larson snapped. "You just might find yourself—"

Steadman turned in the saddle and broke in. "I thought I told you to shut up," he blared. "Now, I mean just that. I'll do the talking."

"I don't know that there's much else to talk about," Chuck told Steadman. "We caught you trying to steal those horses, a herd that belongs to the people of the United States of America. I'll just report what I saw to the BLM detective and he can talk to you. It's their problem."

"You're right," Steadman said with a quick nod. "It's their problem. And you've got no business up here."

"Don't push me, Steadman," Chuck warned. "As it is, you're in pretty deep. I wouldn't make things worse if I were you."

"Do you think you and that dandy there with you got a chance against us?" Steadman asked, pointing to Dan.

Dan held his rifle in his left hand and let his right hand drop to the butt of his Colt revolver. "You'll be the first one down, Steadman," Dan told him. "Just make your play."

Steadman realized immediately that he hadn't scared either Dan or Chuck with his bluff. It was now up to him either to put up or shut up. And as he knew from Dan's eyes that he was a heartbeat away from pulling his pistol, Steadman decided to shake his head.

"Look, I just figured you didn't have to step into things, is all," Steadman said. "I don't see no reason to get sore."

"That's a funny thing to say," Dan told him. "You're the one who thinks you've got the edge. If you think you've got it, use it."

"Listen, we'll just ride on," Steadman said. "I've got a ranch to run and I'm wastin' time with you."

"You ain't goin' to let them run over us like that, are you?" Keith Larson asked from behind.

Again Steadman turned in the saddle. He said nothing, but his look made Larson lower his head.

Steadman finally turned back to Dan and Chuck again. "We'll be leavin' now."

"Expect to hear from the BLM detective, Steadman," Chuck spoke up. "He'll want to ask you some questions."

"I wish you wouldn't do that," Steadman said to Chuck, his tone more a warning than a request.

"You brought it on yourself," Chuck told him. "If I were you, I'd stick to getting stock for my rodeo contracts in a more legitimate fashion."

Steadman took one last look at Chuck and Dan before he turned his horse and waved his men off toward the far end of the meadow. Dan watched them for a while, noting that Chuck was writing notes on a pad of paper. He had obviously recognized most of the men.

Steadman seemed to be taking his time riding off with his men. Chuck finished his notes and turned back for the Jeep. Dan followed him, but didn't have a good feeling about turning his back on Steadman at all, and looked around just in time to see both Nolan Steadman and Keith Larson raise their rifles.

Dan shouted at Chuck and dove for the ground just as the shots echoed. A bullet just missed Dan's left side, but Chuck Farley was not so lucky.

The bullet struck him square in the back, just below the base of his neck, and he was dead before he fell.

Steadman started yelling for his men to finish Dan, and they kicked their horses into a run toward him. Dan knew how badly they wanted him, for he was now a witness to murder. In but a few quick movements, he was back at the Jeep, bullets whizzing past him and into the sagebrush all around his feet.

Steadman and his men kept coming, shooting wildly as they rode. More bullets came and punctured the tires and metal of the Jeep, shattering the glass and headlights and keeping Dan down until they had emptied their rifles.

When Steadman saw that Dan was not going to go down easily, he yelled again for his men to spread out and surround the Jeep from different angles. Dan knew he had to act fast and squirmed out from under the vehicle.

He opened fire with his .30-.30, scattering Steadman and his men in all directions.

His first bullet took a rider moving out to his left from Steadman, sending him sprawling from the saddle and into a heap on the ground. Steadman and the others stared in awe at the shot, knowing they were all sitting ducks for a lawman whose aim was far better than average.

Steadman rounded his men up and waved them into a dash toward the far end of the meadow. Dan wanted Steadman, but the leader was clever enough to keep himself covered by the men who rode with him. Dan knew he had to shoot fast, or they would be out of effective range of his .30-.30.

The outlaw from Montana, Keith Larson, was also riding with men between him and Dan, so Dan decided to take aim at the rider just ahead of Larson.

His rifle cracked and the rider jerked in the saddle and toppled backward off his horse. Larson's horse shied away from the fallen man, throwing Larson to the ground. Larson yelled from the ground, but Steadman wasn't stopping.

Dan ran out toward the yelling Keith Larson, his intention to arrest Larson and take him down to stand trial. But one of the horse hunters turned and rode back to Larson, reaching a hand down. He jerked back as a bullet from Dan's rifle ripped into his side.

Dan levered another round into the barrel of his rifle while Larson pulled the wounded rider down from his horse and took his place in the saddle. Dan had to fall to the ground as Steadman and the other two remaining riders opened fire on Dan once again.

They emptied their guns and spurred their horses for the timber. The last man, just before he reached cover, took a bullet from Dan's rifle low in the side, doubling him down and out of the saddle.

Dan ran past the first horse hunter he had shot and found him dead. The second, who had gone to Larson's aid, tried to rise and fire at Dan, but instead got a blast from Dan's .30-.30 that tore through his chest and knocked him backward and down for good.

When he finally made it to the last wounded rider, Dan moved more cautiously, waiting for an ambush from the trees nearby. The last fallen rider saw Dan's approach and tried to come to his feet. He yelled for Steadman and the others to come back for him. But they were gone, their dust rising through the scrub timber in the distance.

The horse hunter fell back and groaned. Dan walked up to him, his rifle pointed at the rider, and knelt down on one knee. The rider turned and looked up with pain-glazed eyes.

"You've got to get me to a doctor," he said.

Dan turned and pointed back to the Jeep. "You and your friends shot that Jeep up pretty bad, and the tires are flat."

"I mean it, I'm dying," the horse hunter begged.

Dan looked at the man's side, covered with blood that was pouring out from a gaping wound. An internal organ, possibly his liver, had been fragmented by the bullet and bone splinters. He was nearly unconscious and there was no hope of getting him down before he died, even if the Jeep had good tires.

"They left you here to die," Dan told him. "How does that make you feel?"

"Steadman . . . ain't one to care," the horse hunter managed. ". . . He don't care about nothing but that stallion. . . . He wants that stallion."

"Look what it cost you," Dan pointed out. "Where is Steadman's ranch?"

The dying horse hunter shook his head back and forth slowly. "I ain't telling."

"You've got nothing to lose now," Dan said.

"Get Gus and Sadie to help . . . ," the dying horse hunter managed. "Gus and Sadie . . . hate Steadman."

Dan asked him where Gus and Sadie lived, but the rider lost consciousness. There was an exhalation of breath from his lungs and small tremors in his muscles, before he relaxed completely.

The air was beginning to move with an afternoon breeze. The heat of midday was giving way to a coolness from the upper layers of rock and timber along Devil Canyon. Far out in the distance, the herd of wild horses had stopped to graze in an open meadow beside a mountain.

Dan looked out at them for a time and then turned back toward the Jeep. The shock of what had happened was beginning to numb him now.

He walked slowly until he could see where Chuck lay still on his face. He felt the pain and the anger, all at once, and he cursed loudly, swinging the barrel of his rifle against a sagebrush. His yell echoed through the deep canyons of the high country.

He continued the walk back down to his friend, dreading it, but knowing it was something he was going to have to face. He was going to have to go back and tell Chuck's wife that her husband had been killed, and that their son and daughter were now without a father.

Dan finally reached the spot where they had been approaching the Jeep when Steadman opened fire. Chuck was right where he had fallen; not even so much as a finger had moved. Dan knelt down and turned him over, the heavy pull of anguish working at him as he looked into Chuck's lifeless face, something he had never, ever anticipated doing. He blinked back tears.

"I'm sorry, Chuck," he said softly. "I'm so sorry."

He went to the Jeep and found a jacket. It was all there was to cover Chuck with and it would have to do. When he had said a final goodbye to his friend, Dan reloaded his rifle and started the long walk back down to the lake.

THREE

There was a large attendance at Chuck Farley's funeral. Chuck had been well known throughout the northern part of the state, as well as the county. People had gathered from all over, and they were angry.

The media had already gotten their stories and pictures. Dan refused to tell them any more than he could help, as he did not want to give Steadman any idea what was going to happen. But the reporters and interviewers knew full well that Dan intended to go up into the canyons after Steadman. They got information wherever they could on his past and what was likely to happen up above the wild horse preserve.

Dan knew he couldn't keep his picture and the stories out of the paper, and that the headlines would reach out a long way. He knew that Steadman considered himself invincible among those high canyons. But Dan vowed that Steadman's arrogance was going to cost him dearly.

County authorities and the BLM approached Dan immediately after the funeral. Speaking for the county was the county attorney, who told Dan he would arrange to have his salary and expenses paid if he would stay around to help bring Nolan Steadman and the others down to justice.

A BLM detective named Chet Williams and another BLM man named Grover, from Washington D.C., said they were acting on the highest authority when they asked Dan if he would help in the investigation and prosecution of the man responsible for Chuck Farley's death.

"You were up there when it happened," Williams said. "And I've heard there's no one better than you for getting men like Steadman out of the rocks."

Dan was hoping he would get the opportunity at least to help in the investigation. But it sounded as if they were going to give him full control of it.

"We know Steadman will be hard to catch on BLM land from now on," Williams continued. "And the murder was committed on private land. So we will leave the details up to you and offer you any backup you might need."

Dan realized he was going to have to begin by contacting the old couple, Gus and Sadie Wilkins, who owned the land where Chuck was killed. He could remember the dying horse hunter's words about the old couple hating Steadman, and Dan reasoned Steadman must have some kind of hold over them.

These two people would be the key to where to begin looking for Steadman. He had little else to go on, as the bodies of the three horse hunters he had killed were gone when they went up for the

Jeep and Chuck's body.

Williams told Dan that the BLM had very little in their files on Steadman, mainly because the man worked cleverly and there had never been any investigation of him. Rodeo stock contractors who bought his bulls and horses checked brands and other markings, but if everything seemed in order they never asked any more questions.

Steadman had no other record of theft or killing and it amazed Dan to think that a man like that hadn't left a trail a hundred miles long. He had no doubt killed before, and likely often. It didn't bother him at all. He was just clever at hiding evidence.

Based on a lot of things, Dan was sure that Nolan Steadman was going to be a hard man to bring down. Every little detail he could learn about Steadman would be of value.

"It sounds like Steadman has been trouble for some time," Dan said to Williams, "but he just hasn't been caught."

"Up until now, he's chosen to be careful," Williams said. "Maybe he just saw dollar signs when the stallion was set free up there."

Dan asked about the stallion being set free and Williams explained that a stallion from the Colorado back country had been donated by its owner, an elderly lady who was giving her horses away. She wanted the stallion to run free with a wild herd and thus allow his good bloodlines to become infused in future generations, upgrading the class of the wild mustangs.

"He's been after that stallion ever since it was set

loose up there last year," Williams explained. "He won't stop until he's gotten his way, I'm afraid."

"He'll have to stop now," Dan said firmly. "Murder is stepping way over the line."

"He won't be an easy one," Williams warned. "He knows that country up there and he knows how to use it against you. He almost got me one day, and it would have looked like an accident."

Williams went on to explain that he had been investigating a cut fence when Steadman and some of his men showed up. After Steadman had argued over the cut fence, he had left, but had followed Williams later and nearly caused him to drive off a narrow road by rolling a rock down in front of him.

"I never actually saw Steadman do it," Williams said. "But I'm certain it was he."

"I certainly saw him and his horse hunter friends kill Chuck," Dan said emphatically. "He tried his hardest to get me as well. I'm just glad that Jeep of Chuck's was close enough to dive under. I just wish Chuck could have made it . . ."

Dan turned and looked out over the cemetery and into the mountains above town. There was a lot of rough country up there and a lot of treacherous canyons where a false step meant death. It was just the place for a gang of thieves to hide out.

Dan looked back down to where Chuck's wife and family were leaving the grave. The little girl was numb and the boy didn't want to go, but finally turned and stumbled along with his mother, his hand gripping hers tightly, his sobs carrying out beyond the cemetery.

"We'll be ready whenever you want to begin the hunt for Nolan Steadman," Williams said. "We'll take you down to our main office in Billings and you can have all the maps and other supplies you need. We've got a chopper and we can get a SWAT team together when you think the time is right."

"I'll locate them first," Dan said. "That will save a lot of expensive air time. Those canyons can hide men real easy and I doubt if we could locate anyone even from the air without intensive ground backup. I might as well start on the ground and call you guys in when I need you."

Williams nodded. "We'll meet you down in Billings."

"I'll make a few phone calls back to my office in Montana," Dan said. "Then I'll be ready. And I'll stay ready until Nolan Steadman is no longer in those mountains."

It was just past noon when Nolan Steadman came in from the corrals where he had been testing a bucking bronc. He looked for his bottle of whiskey and cursed regularly as he tossed things around and kicked through garbage and refuse on the floor.

There were three chickens on the table, picking at breadcrumbs and other scraps left from various meals. Steadman found his whiskey, then shooed the chickens away and sat down. He reached up on the counter behind him, pulled down a big Colt revolver he had left there, and stuck it down in his lap.

He could hear Keith Larson coming toward the

ranch house. While Larson walked he slapped a morning paper against his thigh and tried to stay ahead of two other hands, who were working to catch up to him.

Steadman smiled, took a swallow of whiskey, and listened. The two hands with Larson were the ones who had survived Dan Slayter's rifle fire three days before. Steadman could hear them arguing as they followed Larson.

"We ain't neither of us staying on," one of them said, a heavy-set man named Nichols. "Trouble is coming up here and we're not staying. Now, we want paid."

"I told you," Larson said with a grunt, "I can't pay you until Nolan gives the go-ahead. You'll have to take it up with him. He's inside."

Now the other man spoke up. He was small and thin, with one bad arm that had been damaged from polio. His name was Whitley.

"Steadman told us to talk to you," Whitley said. "What's all this runaround?"

Larson came into the ranch house and right to the table where Steadman was sitting and drinking from his bottle. He stood over Steadman and thumbed back at the other men.

"These two got something they want to take up with you," Larson told Steadman.

Whitley spoke up. "We want paid for our time. After that shootout with that lawman, we ain't staying up here."

Steadman pointed to the table. "Have a chair, boys, and let's talk about it." He let his right hand fall into his lap.

Steadman took the paper from Larson while Whitley and Nichols sat down. Both men were nervous. Steadman drank from the bottle with his left hand and ignored them while he looked at the front page of the paper.

The headlines in the *Billings Gazette* were big, describing a shooting scene in the Bighorn Mountains, resulting in the death of Sheriff Chuck Farley. Steadman laughed. He threw the paper back across the table at Larson.

"It sounds like that lawman from Montana, that Slayter, is going to come up after us," Larson told Steadman.

Steadman shrugged. "He won't go back alive, either."

"Don't be so damn sure," Whitley spoke up. "That's why we ain't staying. I heard he's a mean bastard."

"No meaner than me," Steadman said, and took a drink. Then he lowered the bottle. "You two ain't getting one dime."

Whitley and Nichols looked at each other and back to Steadman. "That ain't fair," Nichols blurted. "We've worked for you better than a month. We ain't leaving without what's ours."

"Here's what's yours," Steadman said flatly. He pulled his hand up from under the table. He was holding the Colt, and he shot Nichols first.

The bullet tore through Nichols's collarbone and blew a gaping hole in his upper chest. He fell backward off his chair and onto the floor, and began to kick. Whitley stared, unable to believe his eyes. Then Steadman turned the pistol on him and

Whitley yelled.

Steadman fired and hit Whitley in the upper forehead, blowing the back of his head out. Whitley tried to stand up, his eyes dead, but fell forward onto the table and then to the floor.

Setting his bottle down, Steadman rose in his chair and leaned over, inspecting the two men. Whitley was stone-dead, but Nichols was still kicking. He cocked the pistol and put two more bullets into Nichols, one to the back and the other to the head. Then Nichols quit jerking and lay still.

Steadman sat back down and pulled from his bottle.

"Get them out of here," he told Larson.

Larson said nothing, but just stared.

"I said, get them out of here!" Steadman yelled.

Larson got up, dragged the bodies of Whitley and Nichols out, one at a time, and left them in the driveway in front of the ranch house.

When he came back inside, Steadman was reading the paper.

"What do we do with them?" Larson wanted to know.

Steadman never looked up from his paper. "Same as we did with the other three," he answered. "Take them over to the canyon and dump them. Nobody should find them there."

"Maybe we'd ought to bury them," Larson suggested. "All of them."

Steadman didn't look up from the paper this time. "I said dump them in the canyon. We ain't got the time to bury them. Just be sure they fall into the deep part, where nobody can get to."

Larson shrugged. "I just thought it would be better if they were all underground, that's all."

Steadman got up from the table and dumped the empty cartridges from his revolver. He was looking at the paper while he worked with the gun, his eyes intent on Dan Slayter's picture.

"We've got just enough time to round up some more men and get that black stallion before this Slayter character comes up after us," Steadman said. "We've got no time to get worried over whether Nichols and Whitley and the others get buried decent or not. Whitley and Nichols didn't want to stick with us and it wasn't a good idea them just going off, now was it?"

"I didn't say you didn't do the right thing," Larson said quickly.

Steadman kept talking, as if to convince Larson he had made a perfect decision in killing the two men.

"They would have went right down and told where we are up here, wouldn't they? And then there would have been lawmen all over looking for us. I just didn't want that."

"I know, we couldn't let them go," Larson agreed. "I just meant we don't want somebody finding them and knowing who did that, too."

"I'm not going to have trouble with you, too, am I?" Steadman asked.

Larson looked hard at Steadman. "You would have had trouble with me long before now, if you were ever going to have trouble. I want in on the take when we get that stallion."

Steadman nodded. Then he reloaded the revolver and pushed the table over so that it was against the wall. He set the newspaper with Dan Slayter's picture up against the wall and stood back. He fired four times at the paper from point-blank range, again filling the room with smoke. Then he twirled the revolver with his finger by its trigger guard and put the gun back in its holster.

"Let's get Whitley and Nichols dumped," Steadman said. "We've got a lot of work to do."

FOUR

Dan got himself outfitted with a good horse and plenty of rigging to keep his saddle and other tack patched up. He knew that riding the steep canyon country he was headed into was hard on horses and equipment, not to mention riders who took on that responsibility.

He had packed all the food he needed in one bag—most of it dried or easy to fix. He knew he could dig fresh roots and plants that he needed to supplement his diet. He meant to eat light anyway; his stomach wouldn't be quite the same until he got Steadman down from the canyons to justice.

He had the maps and a good radio with him, all he needed to get things done. He intended to get Steadman and his men located before he called in any assistance—there was no need to have everyone spending money for nothing.

Dan took the trails through the canyon country, winding his way up toward the high country. The sun was just above the horizon and the light brought out the yellows and reds in the steep rock walls. The heat would climb in these canyons, Dan knew, enough to cook a man. He would have to be into the higher country by midday, or find himself with his tongue hanging out.

He saw by the map that the Wilkens ranch was about ten miles ahead. The ride was hard and slow. Dan walked part of the way over the roughest and rockiest parts of the trail. He didn't want a lame horse in this country, not when he didn't have an extra with him.

A lot of things ran through his mind as he worked his way ever higher. He couldn't believe that an older couple would be mixed up with a man like Steadman, though you could never tell for sure. A person got surprised every day.

But what seemed more likely was that Steadman was doing what he wanted to whomever he wanted and the Wilkenses happened to be right next door. That made it easy for him to run horses across their property to his and not have any trouble getting a right-of-way. He just took the right of way, and they couldn't stop him.

Near midday he came out of the canyons into higher country and saw that a set of rundown buildings were nestled next to the timber not far ahead. There was a little stream that gurgled out of a draw. That seemed a likely spot to spend the noon hour and learn what was going on between Steadman and the old couple.

He passed a set of rundown corrals adjacent to a log barn. The ranch house stood nearby, surrounded by dust and rabbitbrush plants. On the porch sat an old man and an old woman, rocking lazily, eyeing Dan's approach.

Dan knew this would be Gus and Sadie Wilkens. The couple looked to be nearly seventy, but there could have been five to ten years difference, either way. Time in this country could be hard on a person, or easy, depending on how you used it. As Dan got closer, he could see these two had seen the worst of time.

He was getting close enough to speak when he saw the flash of a rifle barrel in one of the windows.

"Shoot him, Leslie," the old woman said into the house.

Dan pulled his own rifle from its scabbard and jumped down from his horse. The rifle in the ranch house blazed and Dan heard bullets going past him. His horse wheeled and ran off back toward the canyon country.

Gus and Sadie Wilkens continued to rock in their chairs, watching Dan run for cover behind the barn. He looked out from behind the logs and a bullet zinged into the wood near his head.

Dan yelled out to the house, "Hold your fire! I'm a lawman."

There was a silence, broken only by the creaking of the rocking chairs. Finally the woman inside the house spoke.

"How do we know that?" she questioned. "You're a stranger here. You could be anybody."

"If you'll just hold your fire I'll prove it to you," Dan yelled back.

He set the rifle up against the barn and walked out with his hands up. He saw the rifle barrel in the window again, but the barrel was raised, and not pointed at him. Gus and Sadie continued to rock on the porch, watching him closely.

As he got closer, Dan could see through the window that the woman was young, with lots of flowing blond hair. She was not afraid of showing herself, for she held the rifle now so that she could level it easily.

Dan came to a stop and stood easily, his hands still raised. He looked first at the old couple, then to the woman, who was now stepping out onto the porch. In the sunlight, Dan could see that her features were soft and delicate, but that her canyon upbringing had made her as hard as the country. Her blue eyes didn't miss a thing, and with a snap of her head she swung her blond hair back over her shoulders.

She leveled the rifle on Dan once more.

"You're not going to use that, are you?" Dan asked.

"I don't think I'll have to," she answered, "unless you make me."

"My name is Dan Slayter," he said. "I'm up here investigating the murder of Chuck Farley. You heard about that, I'm sure?"

The woman looked at the couple and they shrugged. She turned back to Dan. "We don't hear much up in this country. Take the gun out of your holster and drop it. Do it slow."

"I told you, I'm not here to harm you," Dan insisted. "I just want some information."

"Just do as I say," the woman said. "Then we'll talk. You can't be too careful."

Dan obliged her and then stood waiting for her to decide what she wanted next. Gus and Sadie seemed satisfied that he wasn't going to harm them and nodded to the woman. She lowered the rifle.

"This country don't get many strangers," she told Dan. "You can't just come riding in and m′ yourself at home."

"What are you people afraid of?" Dan askeu.

The old couple just rocked and looked out over the corrals into the hills and canyon country beyond. Behind them, timber covered the rocky slopes, which rolled up into high mountain plateaus.

Dan looked hard at the young woman, who avoided his stare.

"I think I know who you're afraid of," he said. "And that's why I'm here."

She, as well as Gus and Sadie, continued to look the other way.

"You had to know who I was when you saw me riding in," Dan said. "Word gets around in the back country, too. Sometimes quicker than down below. I know; I grew up in the back country."

She flipped her blond hair again and turned quickly to Dan. "Listen, you aren't about to save us from anybody," she said sharply. "We don't want any part of it."

"This is the Wilkens ranch, isn't it?" Dan asked.

The woman nodded. "I'm Leslie and these are my folks, Gus and Sadie. It appears you know a lot about us already."

"That's my job," Dan said. "Don't you have a

twin sister?"

Leslie nodded. "She's out riding. I don't know when she'll be back. She comes and goes as she pleases."

"I need to know some things," Dan went on. "I think you already realize that I'm after Nolan Steadman. I'm wondering how much you know about the death of Chuck Farley. It took place on your land."

"None of that is our concern," Leslie said. She was gripping the rifle tightly now, looking out over the country with her parents.

Dan looked at Gus and Sadie. It was apparent that neither of them was going to say much if they could help it. They continued to ignore him.

Looking at them, Dan became more convinced that they were terrified. Not of him, but no doubt of Nolan Steadman. He had likely been along to tell them to keep their mouths shut about whatever they knew about the horse hunting that was going on.

He had seen this many times before. Down below, in a town or city, Dan could have offered them police protection if they wanted to cooperate. But up here, there was no way to keep them away from Steadman—if he wanted to get them.

"I think it would be good if you could help me," Dan tried again. "Nolan Steadman can't be that good a neighbor."

When he again got no response, he shrugged and turned for the barn to get his rifle.

"I guess I'll go catch my horse and be gone then," he said. "Sorry to have bothered you."

He was walking when Leslie called out to him. "Wait. I'll help you catch your horse."

Dan turned. Gus and Sadie were both glaring at Leslie. It was Sadie who spoke.

"You let him get his own horse."

"I'm the one who scared it off," Leslie replied. "The least I can do is help him catch it."

"Don't go," Gus growled.

"This is our one chance to end all this, and I'm not going to let it slip by," she told the two of them.

"You know what will happen," Sadie said.

"Not this time," Leslie said. "This time things will be different. I know they will."

The old couple turned away from her and she came out from the house toward Dan, carrying her rifle. When she reached him, she pointed to the barn.

"My horse is saddled. Let's just ride out and find yours. He can't have gone far."

"You spooked him with your shooting," Dan acknowledged. "I guess it's a good thing you're a poor shot."

Leslie stopped walking and glared. "You'd best count your lucky stars that I wasn't aiming at you," she said. "I can hit anything I want within three hundred yards."

Dan whistled. "Okay, I believe you. I guess it would be pretty hard to miss me at the distance you were shooting from."

"I could have taken an eye out, had I wanted to," Leslie said. "Don't you forget that."

Leslie went into the barn and led a sorrel mare

41

out. She got into the saddle and put her rifle in a scabbard. Then she offered a hand to Dan.

Dan swung up behind her and gripped the back of the saddle as Leslie kicked the horse into a lope.

"You can hang onto me if you want," Leslie offered. "We might go through some rough country. But just watch your hands."

Dan smiled and wrapped his arms around her middle, careful not to move his hands too high. She was trim and firm and rode her horse as if she had been on its back all her life. She began to talk about their ranch and how hard it was to raise cattle and get them to market so far back in the hills. She said, though, that it was a life she wouldn't give up for any other.

The farther they got away from the ranch house, the more Leslie opened up. She had a distinctly warm and gentle nature under the hard outer cover, and it was obvious to Dan that she needed to talk to somebody about the problems they had been having with Nolan Steadman. But she seemed to want to know a lot about him first, as if seeing for herself that she could trust him.

"If you grew up in the hills, why aren't you still up there?" she asked him.

"The hills are good for solitude," Dan said. "But my life is not built on that. I've got to be around people."

"It seems to me like you're around the wrong people, though, based on the job you've got," she said.

"People like Nolan Steadman are not the majority," Dan pointed out. "That's why it's important to stop those who are like him. It makes things a whole lot easier for everyday folks who just want happiness."

Dan took it upon himself now to try to get her to discuss what was going on with her family and Steadman. He had a pretty good idea, but he just wanted to be sure.

"Is Steadman causing you and your family a lot of problems?" Dan inquired bluntly. "I'll bet he is."

"I can't talk about it," Leslie said. "I just can't talk about any of it."

"You didn't come out here to help me catch my horse if you didn't feel like telling me something."

"I've changed my mind. I can't endanger my parents."

"Nobody has to know you told me anything," Dan said. "Besides, you'll have to answer questions sooner or later. You know that."

"How do I know that?" she asked.

"Because I'm taking him down out of here, one way or another, and whoever has been involved will be questioned by someone. You might as well tell me what's going on."

"You must think you're something," Leslie told him. "There's nobody who has ever been able to stand up to Nolan Steadman."

"The end has come for him," Dan said with conviction. "He's going to have to stand trial for the murder of Chuck Farley—he and the other horse hunters he leads."

"You'll never get Nolan Steadman down out of here," she said. "He knows this country like no other man. And his soul is harder than the rocks in these canyons."

"Chuck Farley was my best friend," Dan said. "My soul is pretty hard right now, too."

Leslie pointed across a little flat to where Dan's horse was grazing. They rode over and Dan got down and caught the horse. Leslie was watching him with interest.

"No, I guess you aren't the ordinary type, are you?" she said. "I guess you would have to either be crazy or really know the hills to come up into this country after Nolan Steadman. Which is it?"

"A little of both," Dan told her.

Leslie looked past Dan to where a rider was moving along the edge of the canyon toward them. Dan could see that Leslie knew who the rider was immediately.

"It looks like my sister has finally decided to come back home," she said.

Dan watched as Sally Wilkens rode her bay horse to a stop next to them and looked from Leslie to Dan.

"You've got a boyfriend?" Sally asked.

Leslie grinned. "Sally, this is Sheriff Dan Slayter, from Montana. Dan, this is my sister, Sally."

Dan tipped his hat. The two women were identical, right down to the length of their hair and the color of their eyes. Dan couldn't even tell that much difference in their voices. He knew he was going to have to look very closely to find something physical to tell them apart.

"Did you say you were a sheriff?" Sally asked Dan, looking him over well.

"That's right. I'm up here to bring Nolan Steadman down the mountain to justice. I understand you know him."

"I know him well enough to be sure he won't let anybody get within rifle range of him," Sally said. "You're taking your life in your hands."

"It wouldn't be the first time," Dan told her.

"I suppose not," Sally said. "But with Nolan, it could be your last."

FIVE

Dan studied Sally Wilkens closely. She was an exact duplicate of Leslie, no question, and he knew he would have to look very closely to find a physical feature that might separate her from her sister.

Like Leslie, her hair was blond and tinged with red, and her mouth had the same soft curves as her sister's. Her body was smooth and slim and with good posture, like Leslie's. But there was one subtle difference that Dan was able to spot.

Sally's left eyebrow had a light streak of red through it, whereas Leslie's was completely blond. From a distance, that slight difference wouldn't count. But up close, he could now tell who was who.

"So, you think I don't stand a chance against Steadman?" Dan questioned Sally. "Does he own this little world up here, or something?"

Sally was still studying Dan, noting his distinct lack of respect for Steadman. She was aware that this man had the hard qualities it took to make a determined manhunter. And since she had read in

47

the paper that Chuck Farley had been a close friend, she knew he would be all the more determined.

"I think you should be afraid of him, yes," Sally finally answered. "I don't know why you would come into a strange country like this and be so confident."

"What makes you think this country is strange to me?" Dan asked. "I feel right at home here." He smiled.

Sally frowned a little, knowing there was going to be no way she could intimidate this man. He was, indeed, someone different. And Nolan Steadman should already know that.

"You should be careful about going out riding by yourself, with a man like Steadman up here," Dan said.

Sally frowned again. "I'm not going to be afraid to go riding now, or at any time. Nobody's going to bother me."

"You're not afraid of Steadman?" Dan asked Sally.

Sally frowned all the harder. "Nolan has always been good to me."

"It seems you know Steadman quite well," Dan said to Sally. "Maybe you could answer some questions for me."

Leslie, who had been listening with interest, now broke in. "No answers to any questions, Sheriff. I already told you that."

"I'm asking your sister," Dan informed her. He turned back to Sally. "What can you tell me about Steadman?"

48

"Nothing that I haven't already told you," she answered. "He eats strangers like you for breakfast." She turned her horse and started off at a lope for the ranch house.

Dan and Leslie watched her leave. Dan got on his horse and prepared to go back to the ranch with Leslie. He was particularly concerned for the Wilkens family now, especially as it appeared that Sally was somehow involved with Steadman.

"She doesn't appear to like seeing me up here," Dan said to Leslie. "Doesn't she realize that Steadman committed a murder, and attempted to kill me as well?"

"I doubt if she's given that much thought, really," Leslie said, reining her horse alongside Dan's. "She thinks she's in love with Steadman."

"She could do better than Steadman," Dan commented. "A lot better."

"You don't understand," Leslie explained. "She thinks Steadman is going to make her a rodeo queen, that he's going to take her all over the country and show her off. He's told her all this. But he's just using her. It will never happen."

Dan nodded. "I see. But that can't stop me from doing my job up here. Steadman committed murder and he'll stand trial for that crime."

Leslie thought for a moment before she let Dan in on a family secret. It wasn't something that could be easily detected, unless you knew both Leslie and Sally very well. But it was important, and Leslie didn't want Dan judging her sister too harshly.

"You should know, I guess, that Sally was hurt

49

in a fall from a horse when she was about ten years old," Leslie said. "The folks didn't take her down to a doctor and she was in a coma for about three days. When she woke up, she couldn't remember anything. She finally came around to almost her real self. But she's never been quite the same since. Do you understand?"

Dan nodded. "I guess I was a bit judgmental at that," he confessed. "But that means you should be watching out for her a little where it comes to making decisions about her life."

"One thing about Sally that hasn't changed," Leslie pointed out, "is that she's always been stubborn as a mule. Just like me. I can't tell her anything she doesn't want to hear."

"Then she's sure Steadman will make her life something wonderful, and nobody can convince her different?" Dan said.

"That's right," Leslie said. "She's made up her mind. What more do I have to say to get through to you?"

Dan shook his head. "I just want to help all of you," he finally said. "Maybe if you tell me what you can about how Steadman has operated, I can put an end to everybody's troubles that much sooner."

"I want you to understand something," Leslie said emphatically. "My parents' lives depend on us keeping what we know about Steadman to ourselves. They've lived in fear of him for years. He helps them make it up here—gives them money now and again—but he demands that they keep still about how he gets the money for them."

"You and your family can't live under Steadman's control for the rest of your lives. You've gone through enough already. It's time to put a stop to it."

Leslie was looking out over the country. Her face was hard now, and she was getting more angry by the second.

"That's easy for you to say," she told Dan. "Just as soon as you're gone, Steadman and his right-hand man, that Larson fellow, will be over here asking us what you wanted, and what my folks told you. They scare my father. My mother yells at them at times. But my father thinks they want to kill him."

Dan was shaking his head. "You've got to stop and think about this: Steadman is slowly killing your parents, whether you want to admit it or not. He's terrorized them to the point that they cannot even think for themselves anymore. You had better decide if you want that to go on or not."

"How am I going to stop it?" Leslie asked.

"I told you, that's why I'm up here," Dan replied. "With your help, I can have Steadman and the others in custody in just a few days' time."

"You're pretty sure of yourself," Leslie told him. "Didn't you hear what Sally said about Steadman, and how he chews everybody up he comes into contact with?"

Dan allowed himself a little smile, a smile that Leslie saw. He pointed into the high country.

"I grew up on a mountain like that one way up there," he told Leslie. "I don't care who Nolan Steadman thinks he is—he's not going to get away from me. I've come up after him, and I intend to take him back down with me—one way or another."

Leslie looked at Dan closely. "Yes, I believe you're right," she finally said. "I think you will do that. But I don't want you hurting my sister or my parents."

"I need your help, then," Dan told her. "I can't talk to your sister—you'll have to do that. But I want you to see if your folks won't cooperate some with me."

"That will be hard," Leslie said. "I've already told you, they're awfully afraid."

Dan was going to ask why they hadn't moved out. But he realized that a couple as old as they were had no place else to go, and that they were so rooted here that moving them would likely kill them emotionally. But getting them out of there at least until Steadman was gone was a good solution.

"Why don't you let met take you and your folks down off this mountain until we get Steadman?" Dan asked. "Everything will be safe once he's behind bars."

"You couldn't drag them down from here," Leslie said. "Not unless you killed them first."

They rode over the hill above the ranch and Dan saw that both Gus and Sadie were standing on the porch, looking up the hill at them.

"They don't like this at all," Leslie told Dan. "I'll go talk to them alone for a while."

At the bottom of the hill, Dan rode to the corrals and watered his horse. He watched while Leslie got down from her horse in front of the porch. A heated argument ensued, and finally Leslie hurried to the water trough to talk to Dan.

"I'm sorry, Sheriff Slayter," Leslie said as she stopped in front of him. "My folks want me to ask you to ride out. They don't want any trouble here. I have to ask you, please, not to make them more uncomfortable."

"I'm afraid it's too late to worry about that," Dan told her. "Steadman already knows I'm here. The safest thing for all of you is to just sit tight and let me help you. I'm going to radio for men to come up here first thing in the morning."

"They don't want that," Leslie said. "Don't you understand? They just want you to leave."

Dan looked over to where the old couple were now seating themselves in their rocking chairs. He was going to have to tell the old couple that he now had no choice but to stay and finish the job he came up to do. He would go down and talk to them and try to make them understand, but he knew they wouldn't like it in the least.

"I'll go talk to them," Dan said. "I thought maybe this would end up like it has, and I'm sorry it did. But there would have been just as much—if not more—trouble had I decided not to stop here first. Steadman knows that sooner or later you, your sister, and both your parents would all be involved one way or another."

"I knew we would all be involved," Leslie admitted. "I just didn't know it would be this deep."

"It seems to me that they got themselves

involved about as deep as they could get even before I showed up here," Dan pointed out. "It's not my fault that Steadman chose to kill Chuck Farley."

Leslie was trying to understand why Dan was being so adamant about his position. She realized he wasn't going to take no for an answer.

"You're pretty hard about this," she said. "What if something happens to me or my folks?"

"You have to understand," Dan explained. "I'm looking at it from Steadman's point of view. You and your family know a lot about Steadman already. He's not going to let that go by. He would figure to kill you all sooner or later anyway. He couldn't afford to take the chance that you might tell what you know in a court of law. I've got no choice but to stay here and protect you and your folks. I'm sorry if it's an inconvenience, but I can't help it."

Dan walked past her toward the house. She hurried and caught up with him, but said nothing more as they neared the porch.

Dan stopped with Leslie where the old couple rocked together. Gus and Sadie weren't going to talk to Dan at all, but he made them stop and think with the first thing he said.

"You two must think I came up here to sightsee or something. If I'm going back down, you two are coming with me. Then you can stand trial for aiding and abetting a criminal."

It was Sadie who spoke up in a gravelly voice. She turned to Dan as she sat in her rocker, and her eyes were narrowed.

"Where do you get off with that, Sheriff?" she asked. "We ain't no criminals."

"You've allowed Nolan Steadman to do what he's wanted to up here for some time. And some of his lawbreaking ways have taken place on your property. That makes you two just as guilty as he is."

"You ever looked into that man's eyes and told him no to something?" It was Gus who spoke this time, and he was angry.

"It's time somebody did," Dan pointed out. "And that's why I'm here. As long as I can work to get him down from this country, you people won't have to tell him anything ever again."

"You make it sound so simple," Leslie put in. "Just how are we supposed to be so sure that you can stop Steadman?"

"It doesn't have to be just me," Dan said. "Didn't you ever think that you could all work together with me to put an end to this? Why have you allowed him to make you think you couldn't do anything to stop him, ever?"

"He kills for sport," Gus said. "We ain't got a chance if he decides he don't like us."

"What ever made you think he liked you?" Dan asked. "Sooner or later, whether I showed up or not, he would decide you people knew too much about him. I've come up here to help you understand that and put an end to his marauding ways."

Gus and Sadie were thinking hard, eyeing Dan and working their rockers back and forth. They realized what he was telling them made sense. But it was hard to face the fact that they were prisoners to a killer on their own land.

"I'm going to radio down into Lovell and have men sent up here by early tomorrow," Dan went on. "They'll be staying on until Steadman is out of your lives."

It was Leslie who spoke up. "I want you to promise me you'll do everything you can to keep Steadman away from here," she said. "If he ever knew this was happening, he wouldn't blink an eye when he shot us."

"What about Sally?" Sadie asked. "She ain't back yet. If she don't come home, I'll worry myself sick."

Dan thought about it for a moment before he spoke. "I don't know what to tell you about that," he finally said. "I just hope she comes to her senses before too much longer."

SIX

Steadman and Keith Larson had been riding since dumping the bodies into the canyon. Plans had changed in a short while and as Steadman had told Larson before, there was going to have to be an all-out effort made to capture the stallion and get out of the area for a while.

They were now just crossing the line into Montana to find the rest of the horse-hunting gang. The other members of the gang had been getting ready to come back down to the main ranch in the Bighorn Mountains. They had pretty well selected the best horses from the Pryor Mountain herd and were ready to tell Steadman how to go about getting them.

Instead, Steadman and Larson rode into their camp late in the evening, surprising them. The air was cool and the high country was dripping from a recent thunderstorm. Steadman had already worked things out wiht Larson about what was to be said, and Steadman called them all together around a large campfire.

"What's going on down there at the main

ranch?'' one of the men asked Steadman. His name was Claude Mosely. He was a big man, with heavy, dark features and an unerring air for detail. Steadman had placed him in charge of this group sent to the Pryors.

Mosely was holding a small battery-powered radio. ''It sounds to me like you and the others had some kind of shootout with the law,'' he said. ''A bad shootout.''

''We had the black stallion and they scared him off,'' Steadman said. ''Then they opened fire on us. We didn't have much choice.''

''There's going to be a lot of lawmen after you,'' another man said to Steadman. ''That don't sound good. Where does that leave us?''

''That's why we're here,'' Steadman replied. ''We've got to get that black stallion right away now, and get him out of the area. I can deal with the rest of it, but I need that stallion as soon as we can get him.''

''Did you get him off the range, like you said you were going to?'' Mosely asked.

''We got him off,'' Steadman said with a nod. ''Now, all we have to do is get him into the box canyon and we'll have it all done. Then everyone can smile.''

Mosely spoke up again, going back to the news he had heard several times over the radio.

''The news has it that three of our men got shot up. Who got shot?''

Steadman went through his version of what had happened, including the attempt to get Dan Slayter. ''Chuck Farley and that Montana lawman

58

opened up on us and took out Brice, Wilson, and Carlson before we could even blink. Keith and I finally got Farley, but that other lawman, that Slayter, hid under their Jeep. We had to get out of there."

"What about Nichols and Whitley?" Mosely asked. "Why ain't they with you tonight?"

"They both quit yesterday and they're gone," Steadman replied with a straight face. "Up and quit. Said they was scared and didn't want to go to jail."

Larson didn't even blink an eye at the mention by Steadman that Nichols and Whitley had left on their own. He had put the bodies into a canyon so deep that even the vultures couldn't find them.

"What if they tell the law about all of us?" Mosely asked.

Steadman and Larson looked back and forth to one another. Finally, Steadman said, "I told them if they did a fool thing like that I'd hunt them down and they'd wish they'd never been born. They said they was headed south and wouldn't stop until they hit Arizona."

Mosely shrugged and then nodded. "That leaves us short, and we need all the men we can get."

"We're short men, but we'll get by," Steadman said. "We ain't got time to worry about it now. We've got to catch that stallion and get him down out of the mountains."

"What about the plans for the horses here?" Mosely asked. "We've spent some time getting this figured out."

"We'll just have to wait on these horses,"

Steadman said. "That stallion is most important now, and we've got to get him before the law comes up."

"The law is already up, the way I hear it on the radio," Mosely stated. "Who's this Dan Slayter, this sheriff from Montana? From the news, it sounds like Chuck Farley was his best friend. And it sounds like this Slayter is somebody to be reckoned with."

"Do you believe everything you hear?" Steadman asked Mosely. "You turning yellow on me, too?"

"No, but I've got a feeling about this one," he replied. "I don't know that I'd want this guy on my trail."

Steadman put his hands on his hips. "Are you saying you want to quit?"

Everyone was quiet while Mosely contemplated his answer. The wood in the fire popped and cracked while everyone waited. Finally, Mosely shook his head.

"No, I guess not. I'm in past my neck already. No call to pull out now."

"Anyone else worried about this Montana sheriff?" Steadman asked the others.

No one else spoke up and Steadman concluded that everyone was going to remain with him. He finished his coffee, took the pot off the fire, and threw its contents out into the night beyond camp. Everyone stared, but no one spoke.

"I'm running this show and I don't want anyone to forget that," Steadman told the silent bunch. "I've worked a long time to get where I'm at and I want that stallion bad. And I'm going to have him. Montana sheriff or not, I'm going to get that black stallion and haul him down south and start a herd with him. We can all profit from that. Is there anyone who doesn't agree?"

Again there was silence.

"Good," Steadman finally said. "Let's break camp and get back to the Bighorns. Come first light, we're going to be after that stallion."

Dan lay on his bedroll in the Wilkens's barn. He had been afforded a place to stay by Gus and Sadie. It had taken some time and determination to get them to understand what they were up against, but they finally had come to understand that he was there to keep harm from coming to them.

Earlier in the evening, Dan had radioed down from the mountain and had been in touch with the sheriff's office in nearby Lovell, Wyoming. They in turn were going to notify the BLM detective, Williams, that Dan needed a team of experienced deputies right away. Williams was to get in touch with him as soon as possible.

Dan wondered how long that was going to take. It sounded as if Williams had gone out on some important business and was tied up. But the dispatcher realized that the Steadman case took priority over everything else and told Dan she would certainly find Williams as soon as possible and have him get back in touch.

Meanwhile, a party of deputies was starting out from Lovell at first light. They would assist in watching the Wilkenses and keeping Steadman from causing them harm. Dan knew he was making targets of Gus and Sadie Wilkens, and possible Leslie as well.

Before turning in, Dan had noticed that Sally's horse was still gone. She was no doubt on her way to warn Steadman. It would be only a matter of time until Steadman showed up to see what was going on. And he would want to end things right away if he could.

The one thing that Dan thought might keep Steadman from coming to the Wilkens place right away would be the stallion. He had successfully gotten the herd off the wild horse range down below and it was certain he wanted to catch the stallion as quickly as possible. The more time he wasted, the less chance he would have at the horse.

Dan knew that the way to stop Steadman for sure was to locate the stallion and his herd. But Gus and Sadie Wilkens were in danger as long as Steadman was on the loose, and their lives were the most important.

He thought more about how he could stop Steadman and still keep things safe at the Wilkens ranch. Even with men watching, he didn't want Steadman coming and causing trouble.

What he needed to know was definitely where the herd was now and how far it was from the Wilkens ranch. It would be good to get a helicopter to locate the herd for him and possibly Steadman and his horse hunters. It would be hard to hold Steadman and his men in the rough country without experienced riders, but they would have to do the best they could under the circumstances.

But nothing could happen at all until he got in touch with Williams. He lay with his radio on, hoping that a broadcast would come across soon.

Dan was just getting to sleep when he heard footsteps just outside the door. He pulled his pistol from its holster next to him and carefully climbed out of the bedroll and behind the cover of a feed trough.

He was ready to cock the hammer back when he heard one of the twins calling to him.

"Sheriff Slayter, it's Leslie. Can I come in?"

Dan relaxed and told her to come ahead. She came in and turned aside just a little while he pulled his pants on in the shadows.

"I hope I'm not disturbing you," Leslie said.

"Not at all," Dan assured her. "Is everything all right?"

"I just thought I needed to talk to you about what you said this afternoon," Leslie began. "My folks are really worried now that Steadman has killed Chuck Farley and you're here. They're sure Steadman will come soon and wonder if we've told you all about his operation."

Dan could tell from Leslie's voice that she was scared. It was certain that she was right, that Steadman would be wondering what kind of evidence the Wilkenses would be able to show against the gang of horse hunters.

Of course, the Wilkens ranch had a lot of knowledge about Steadman and his operation. There was the possibility that Steadman might think they knew too much. Dan had been thinking about that, and the solution was clear.

"I have decided to have men brought up here to protect your family," Dan finally said. "Once Steadman and the others are in custody, you won't have to worry."

"Will they be able to keep Steadman away from us?" Leslie asked.

"They will be here all the time," Dan promised. "I will radio in again the first thing in the morning. And I'll wait until they get here before I go after Steadman."

Leslie seemed relieved. But she was still nervous. In the moonlight that came in through one of the barn windows, he could see the concern on her face.

She came toward him and he took her in his arms. She cried softly for a short time.

"I just know that Steadman is going to come here and try and kill us all," she said.

"He just wants me," Dan said, trying to console her. "Nobody is going to get hurt."

She cried some more, then finally backed away from him and apologized.

"There's nothing to be sorry for," Dan assured her. "Steadman is someone to be afraid of. There's a lot of pressure on you right now, and no one's going to think you're weak for being emotional. Just don't hold anything back from me that might help me get Steadman sooner."

"I'm afraid for Sally," Leslie said. "I'm almost sure she's so involved with him that she won't use common sense. I don't know what will happen to her."

"Hopefully, she'll return and you can talk her into staying here," Dan suggested. "That's all you can hope for."

"He won't let her go," Leslie said. "He surely won't, not if he knows you're here. And she'll tell him that for sure. Then he'll come here to the ranch and all my nightmares will come true." Her voice showed she was more nervous now than ever.

"You could cause some nightmares of your own with that rifle you shot at me with earlier," Dan told her. "Did you ever have to shoot at a man with it?"

"I thought about shooting Steadman a number of times," Leslie said. "But I could never make myself even point the thing at him."

"You didn't have any trouble with me," Dan said. "Why is Steadman so special?"

"Because, if you look in his eyes, you can see that he kills because he likes to," she answered. "I knew I couldn't pull the trigger on him, aiming right at him. I couldn't shoot right at you, either. But in the same situation, Steadman would have turned around and killed me—even if Sally is my sister."

"Then you had better not stay up here," Dan warned her. "You had better find a way to talk your folks into going down off this mountain with you until I can get Steadman. If you stay up here, you might need to point that rifle at him and make him hold his ground—and be ready to protect your family and property if he comes at you."

"There are some good locations in these hills around here, that overlook the ranch," Leslie said. "You could show them to the men who are coming up here. If there were enough men on the hills around here, Steadman couldn't even get down to the ranch."

"I want you to show me those locations," Dan said. "First thing in the morning."

Leslie looked into his eyes once more before she left. Dan could see that she was wishing she didn't have to wait until morning to show hm the hills around the ranch. But she smiled and walked slowly toward the door and turned.

"I'll see you in the morning, then," she said. "I feel better already."

SEVEN

Sally got to Steadman's ranch well after midnight, just after he and the rest of his men had returned from the Pryor Mountains. She was now convinced that this sheriff, Dan Slayter, was going to be a lot of trouble. She didn't want that.

There was only one way to make sure that the man she cared for knew about it, and that was to warn him.

Steadman and his men were unsaddling their horses when he heard her coming. He was surprised to see her and wondered what could bring her to his place so late. He was used to her coming and staying a few days at a time. But this was the first time she had arrived in the middle of the night—and out of breath.

There was no electricity at Steadman's ranch and he had a number of kerosene lanterns burning. Some of Steadman's men watched Sally approach and held rifles ready until Steadman was sure who it was riding in so late at night.

"I had to get over here and warn you," Sally told Steadman, jumping down from her horse. "That sheriff is over at our ranch, and he's going to come looking for you."

"Is that all you're worried about?" Steadman said. "I thought maybe it was something important."

"You ought not to be that way. He's not like everybody else," Sally warned.

"No, he's not," Steadman acknowledged, throwing his saddle over a pole in the barn. "But he bleeds the same way as everybody else. He's going to end up like his buddy did the other day." He began to rub his horse down with a section of blanket.

"They'll just send more lawmen up after you," she said, watching him rub the horse down. "Why don't we just move out of these mountains and into some other area?"

Steadman stopped working with his horse and looked hard at Sally. "Don't you ever tell me what I should do," he warned. "I'm not afraid of no petty sheriff and he ain't going to run me out of nowhere."

"I just thought you should know," Sally said defensively.

"Hell, I know he's up here," Steadman said, going back to work. "And I'll bet your folks are telling him everything they know."

"That's not what they're doing," Sally assured him. "They're not telling him anything. And they want him to leave."

"They want him to *leave?*" Steadman asked with surprise. "You mean, they're letting him use their place as headquarters?"

68

"It was Leslie's idea," Sally said. "She told him he could stay in the barn."

Steadman laughed. "Leslie must need a man real bad."

Though she thought she cared a lot about Steadman, Sally took offense at the remark about her twin sister. Leslie didn't have it in mind to go after the sheriff romantically, she thought, but merely to help keep their folks safe. That was her main cause, and she didn't like Steadman making fun of it.

"Leslie could get anyone she wanted if she really tried," Sally finally told Steadman.

Steadman was nearly finished rubbing his horse down, and now had a currycomb, getting briars and stickers out of the horse's coat.

"I'm not concerned about that one way or the other," he said flatly. "I want that black stallion and that sheriff is standing in the way. That's how I see it. If your folks are helping him, then they're in the way, too."

"But I told you, they're *not* helping him," Sally protested. "He just showed up and now he's there. He just took over."

Steadman finished with his horse. He was silent, and Sally knew he was wondering whether or not to believe her. But there was no reason he shouldn't believe her; there was no way her folks would cross Steadman—they were scared to death of what he might do.

Sally watched as the last of Steadman's men left the barn, leaving her alone with him. They had all put their horses up in a hurry. They knew they would be afforded only a few hours' sleep before Steadman had them up and after the black stallion.

But Keith Larson had overheard a lot of what Sally had been saying to Steadman, and he walked over to Steadman.

Steadman was talking with Sally, glad to hear of Dan Slayter's whereabouts.

"Maybe it's a good thing that Slayter fellow is staying at your place," Steadman was saying. "That way we know where he is. We're going to catch that stallion tomorrow."

"Maybe we'd ought to take care of that sheriff first," Larson advised. "We can send a few men with Mosely up to watch the stallion and his herd, while the rest of us finish that sheriff. Then we won't have to worry about him."

Steadman looked at Larson and considered the thought. "That does make sense," Steadman finally said. "That would let us work the stallion without worry. It wouldn't be nothing to smoke him out of that barn."

"I'm worried about my folks," Sally said. "They'd be in the way."

"You can see to it they stay inside their little house and don't come out," Steadman said. "There's just the one lawman, Slayter, isn't there?"

"That's all I saw," Sally answered. "He was riding with Leslie when I talked to him."

"How much has she told him?" Larson wondered aloud.

"I already told Nolan that there's no worry," Sally snapped at Larson. She didn't particularly care for him and she wasn't about to let him butt in on their discussion about her family.

"I was just wondering," Larson said. "We've got to be real careful now."

"You just don't worry about my sister," Sally said again.

"Go bring the men back in here," Steadman told Larson.

"They're likely asleep," Larson said.

"Then wake them up!" Steadman blared.

Larson nodded and hurried out of the barn toward the bunkhouse. Steadman watched him leave and turned back to Sally.

"I think I'll go back," Sally said. "I'll see if I can get my folks to leave tonight."

Steadman shook his head. "Not a chance, Sally. You want to tip off that lawman? You just worry about your folks when we get to the ranch. We ain't after them—not yet, anyway."

"I told you, they haven't been telling that lawman anything," Sally repeated. She was almost in tears.

Steadman chuckled. "I was just funnin' you, is all," he finally said. "We ain't after your folks. You can go and be with them while we get rid of that sheriff."

Larson returned with the men and Steadman explained his plan to get rid of Dan Slayter. He discussed the idea that Claude Mosely take four men and go up into the canyon country and keep an eye on the stallion and his herd, while the rest of them went to the Wilkens ranch and got rid of Slayter. Then they would all meet on Mexican Hill to go after the stallion.

The men went back to the bunkhouse and Larson stayed behind for a while.

"I want to be sure and get that lawman," Larson told Steadman. "He's the only one who was there to see us with those horses, and see Chuck Farley go down."

"You'll be with me," Steadman told him. "If you shoot good, you just might be the one to drop him."

"I aim to do what it takes to get him," Larson vowed. "I'll shoot his horse, anything, just so we get him."

"Go on up to the bunkhouse," Steadman told Larson. "Get them all up in three hours. Got that? We need a couple of hours to get to the Wilkens place and get set."

Larson was out the door and Sally was looking at Steadman with concern. "You want to go and get that sheriff in the morning, but will you be careful of my folks?"

"I already told you, your folks will be fine. Just so they don't get in the line of fire."

"What about Leslie?"

"Same with her. She ain't in no danger, either. It's just that sheriff. I have to stop him, or he'll see me in jail for the rest of my life."

"What about me when this all happens?" Sally asked him. "You won't let me tell my folks what you want to do."

"You just ride with me and wait until it's all over," Steadman told her. "Then you can go to your folks. Things will be quiet then."

"You sure?" she asked.

"I'm sure."

Steadman put his arm around her and started walking, ushering her out of the barn toward his house. Sally was by now used to his forcefulness, and it had gotten to be something she needed. Steadman had been making most of her decisions for her for the last two years, and she was at the point that she couldn't make them herself very well. Steadman liked it that way.

"And I've got other things to talk to you about," Steadman added. "You want to be a rodeo queen, don't you?"

"Yes, Nolan, you know that," she answered.

"Good. We can talk a little bit about getting you entered in the NILE Rodeo as a queen contestant," Steadman told her. "Wouldn't you like that?"

"That would be nice," Sally said. "Real nice."

Steadman nodded and pulled her closer to him. Then he stopped and kissed her roughly. "Let's go in," he said. "I'm glad you came tonight."

It was just at dawn when Dan rolled from sleep and, within minutes, was saddling his horse. As a pink-crimson light spread across the canyon country, Leslie came down to the barn from the house and watched him for a time, the caught her own horse.

"Are you going riding someplace?" Dan asked her.

"With you, wherever you're going," she answered.

"Don't you think you ought to watch your folks?"

"I know you're not going far," she said. "I just

73

want to be close to you today, to maybe help you with whatever might happen."

"What do you think is going to happen?" Dan asked, tightening the cinch.

"I didn't sleep too well," she told Dan. "I don't like the feeling around here this morning. My horse is skittish."

"I'm a stranger," Dan said. "Do you think that has something to do with it?"

Leslie shrugged. "Maybe. But I'm just not sure."

"The deputies from Lovell should be on their way by now," Dan said. "I intend to go up on the hill where I was last night and radio down. The people down there will be able to tell me when the deputies left, and that will give me a better idea when they should get here."

"I'm going to stick with you, wherever you go," Leslie said. "You don't mind, do you?"

Dan smiled. "I don't mind one bit."

Dan and Leslie mounted their horses and rode toward a patch of timber atop a nearby hill where Dan had radioed down the evening before. The sun was now just above the horizon and it bathed the steep rock cliffs in thin layers of light yellow and gold. Already the day was showing signs that the heat in the canyons would be enough to make the rocks into hotplates.

"I hope those deputies got a real early start," Dan told Leslie. "Otherwise they're going to be riding up through a dry heat sauna."

Leslie wasn't listening. She was turned, looking into the trees just a way along the ridge. She suddenly stood up.

"There's somebody over there," she said, pointing.

Dan was just getting ready to put the radio to his mouth. Instead, he stood up as well and turned, just as a shot was fired from the trees.

The bullet struck the radio in his hand, just in front of his chest, shattering it and numbing Dan's whole arm. He ran for his horse and managed to throw the reins over and climb on as a hail of gunfire erupted from the trees.

Leslie was already on her horse, headed down the slope toward the barn. Dan had just gotten into the saddle when a bullet punctured the left lung of his horse. Though his arm still tingled, he manged to grab his rifle and step from the saddle as the horse plunged head-first into the grass.

Dan knew who had come to get him, and now Steadman and his men had a good chance of doing just that.

He took position behind the dying horse, levering a round into the barrel of his rifle. He had to remain back a short distance from the wheezing animal; its hooves were flying wildly, as the animal kicked out the last heartbeats of its life.

Dan stayed low as more gunfire sent bullets across the ridge at him. He couldn't rise up enough to get any shots off himself, and had to be content to stay down and wait for Steadman and the others to show themselves.

Dan wondered why Steadman and the others didn't come out from the trees at least to circle around him. But he realized the reason when he saw Leslie shooting into the trees from where she had taken position on another nearby ridge.

Finally, the horse lay still and Dan crept up under its stomach. On the hill, Steadman and his men were finally spreading out, preparing to come across at him. A few riders could be seen moving out of the cover of the trees, opposite where Leslie was shooting, to begin the assault.

Dan leveled his rifle and dropped one of them from the saddle, and the others rode back into the trees. For now, he was safe behind the horse. But he knew the standoff couldn't last forever. He was vulnerable where he was and stood no chance of making it if he tried to run for better cover.

As it was, Steadman was reorganizing his men and they would be coming down at him in just a short while. He only hoped that between his rifle and Leslie's they could hold Steadman and his men off for as long as it took the deputies to ride up from Lovell.

The minutes seemed like hours to Dan as Steadman planned the assault once again. Steadman felt he had no reason to hurry, and he wanted to be sure to get Dan before he left. Dan was trapped where he was now, and it would be only a matter of time until it was over.

Dan watched for riders coming out of the trees on the hill again. Sooner or later they would have to break from their cover in order to reach him. The angle was such now that they couldn't shoot down the ridge over the dead horse and get him— they were only wasting their ammunition.

And with Leslie's sure shooting from the other

hill nearby, they were going to have to be careful how they made their attack.

Then, from his position behind the dead horse, Dan suddenly saw a line of riders led by Keith Larson come racing out of the trees along the ridge toward him. Going the other direction was Sally, headed right for Leslie.

And going downslope toward the ranch house, right through the middle, was Steadman.

Dan couldn't get an angle on Steadman, as Larson and the others began pouring bullets at him as they held their horses up at a distance. Dan realized they didn't care whether or not they hit him, as they were merely covering Steadman as he rode down the hill to the ranch house—where he no doubt intended to make hostages of Gus and Sadie Wilkens.

EIGHT

Steadman rode as hard as he could toward the ranch house. He was nearly to the barn now and felt his chances of making it were way better than even. His men had Dan Slayter pinned behind his horse and Sally and Leslie were now fighting over Leslie's rifle. Neither Dan Slayter nor Leslie would be able to get a good shot off at him.

He had come to the ranch with Keith Larson and just over half of his men. Claude Mosely had the rest of the men up in the high country looking for the black stallion and the wild herd of mustangs. Killing two birds with one stone was Steadman's idea, but he didn't think it would take the effort it was now demanding.

He had Keith Larson to blame for that. Larson had opened up at too great a distance and though he would have hit Dan Slayter dead center, Slayter had moved and the bullet had smashed into his radio. Had everyone been closer, they all could have opened up and finished him. As it was now, everything was going to be a lot more difficult.

Sally was going to be hard to deal with now as

well. She had insisted on coming along to watch the lawman die, as she was worried about her folks. He had told her repeatedly that her folks would not be involved. But plans change, Steadman thought to himself, and she would just have to understand.

She had no idea he was going to be riding down to the ranch house. He had told her that he was going across the ridge with the others after Dan Slayter, and that she should ride over and keep her sister, Leslie, occupied so that there would be no gunfire from her.

The plan had worked well and now Steadman was nearing the house. He had told Keith Larson and the others to stay out of Slayter's range; he was deadly with that rifle. They were to keep him pinned down and then go back into the trees and wait for it all to be over. He didn't want Dan Slayter shooting any of his men and he knew that when he had the old couple as hostages, Dan Slayter would come down to help them.

Larson had argued that they should try to get Slayter any way they could, that something could go wrong. But Steadman wanted the lawman for himself and told Larson to wait up in the trees with the others as he was told. He couldn't afford to lose any more men if the sheriff opened fire.

As he rode past the barn, Steadman began to laugh. Sally was coming down the hill on her horse, yelling out to him. She wanted to know what he was doing. Just across from her and up the slope, he could see Leslie riding over to pick up Dan Slayter. He watched the lawman quickly jump up behind her on her horse, and they rode down toward him.

Steadman was still laughing. They were too late to stop him now.

Steadman jumped from his horse to the porch and broke through the door into the house. Sadie was holding a butcher knife in her hand and Gus was trying to load a rifle—an old .50-caliber Sharps from his collection. He had hoped to get a longer shot at Steadman.

"What have we got here?" Steadman said with a laugh. "Drop that buffalo gun, old man."

Gus tried to hurry to get the bullet into the rifle. Steadman realized his intention was serious, but knew that if he killed the old couple he wouldn't have a chance of getting Dan Slayter. Instead, he fired a shot into the floor at Gus's feet.

"I said drop the rifle!"

Gus reluctantly let the old Sharps slip from his fingers. He held his shaking hands above his head, while Sadie continued to hold the knife.

Steadman rushed at Sadie and she slashed awkwardly at him. Angered, Steadman raised his pistol and aimed it at her head. She quickly dropped the blade and cowered. He fired just over her head and she yelled. Then he backhanded her and she fell to the floor.

"What did you do that for?" Gus asked. "What are you hurting us for? You came after the sheriff."

Steadman grabbed Gus by the collar. He put the barrel of his revolver to the old man's head.

"Let's go to the window, old man."

Suddenly Sally rushed into the house, and

looked at Steadman with horror. She expected to find her parents dead. She was relieved to see them still alive.

Leslie came in behind her and gasped. Sadie still lay on the floor, recovering from the blow, while Steadman pushed Gus in front of him toward the window.

"You two just stay out of the way," Steadman ordered. "That way nobody gets hurt."

"What are you doing, Nolan?" Sally asked. "You promised."

"I had no choice!" Steadman yelled at her. "Now, get back out there and take your sister with you." He ordered Leslie to leave her rifle behind on the floor.

Leslie dropped the rifle and Sally came forward. "You told me they wouldn't be involved," she shouted, pointing to her folks. "And now you've hurt them."

"I said get back out there!"

Steadman clamped his forearm under Gus's chin and held him while he pushed Sally hard toward the door. Sally fell down and looked at Steadman before starting to her feet. Steadman had his pistol pointed at her father's head.

Sally's face flushed with anger. "You liar! You've always lied to me, haven't you? I ought to kill you."

"Just settle down," Steadman ordered. "I told you I wanted you and your sister outside. I mean it."

Sally had her hands doubled into fists and Leslie cautioned her against doing anything foolish.

Leslie went over to Sadie, who was now rising to her hands and knees.

"Stay away from her," Steadman ordered. "Go outside with your sister and tell Slayter I want him to come in here."

Leslie got her mother to her feet and Steadman yelled at her, then fired his pistol over her head. She jumped.

"I want you and Sally to go outside now," Steadman ordered again.

Sally came toward Steadman once more. "We aren't leaving our folks," she said firmly.

"Do as he says, Leslie," Gus managed to say. ". . . Just do as he says."

Leslie came over from where she had stabilized Sadie against the kitchen table. Sally didn't want to go, but Gus again told them to go out, that things would work out. The two of them backed slowly out the door, fearful of leaving their parents yet certain they had no choice.

Steadman was now in front of the window with Gus and he could see Dan Slayter levering a bullet into his rifle. Steadman then broke the window glass and shouted out into the ranch yard.

"Drop the rifle, Slayter. Then I want you to come in here."

Dan held his rifle ready to level and fire. Steadman watched him and licked his lips.

"You're not listening to me," Steadman yelled out to Dan. "I'm not going to give you any more time. I'll kill these two now, if that's what you want."

Steadman was laughing again. He knew there

was no way Dan Slayter could do anything but what he was ordered. He yelled again and heard the sheriff say he wanted to see both Sadie and Gus, so that he knew they weren't dead.

"They're alive," Steadman insisted. "You know that."

"Maybe they're badly hurt," Dan yelled back. "You bring them out here and prove to me that they aren't nearly dead. Because if they are, you don't stand a prayer in hell."

Steadman turned from the window and yelled at Sadie to get outside to the porch. He had his forearm again clamped under Gus's chin, and Gus was gagging as Steadman dragged him along.

Sadie put an arm up as Steadman raised his hand to hit her again. She managed to stumble out the door onto the porch, where he pushed her to her knees.

Then he put his revolver to Gus's head once more.

"Here they are, Slayter," Steadman yelled. "Now, I want you to get over here, or watch me put bullets into them."

He watched while Leslie walked up to where Dan stood with his rifle. She was talking to him, pointing to her folks, her whole body trembling with fear.

"Did you hear what I said, Slayter?" Steadman yelled.

"I heard you," Dan called back.

"Then drop that rifle and do as you're told."

Dan acted as if he'd never heard the order. Instead, he raised his rifle and aimed it at

Steadman's head.

"What are you doing?" Leslie asked him.

"You think he's going to be charitable?" Dan asked her. "He'll kill us all. I can't let him do that."

"Put the rifle down, Slayter!" Steadman yelled again. He licked his lips harder and put the pistol tightly under Gus's chin.

"You go ahead and shoot him, Steadman, then you'll die for sure," Dan promised. He was holding his rifle ready to fire.

"No," Leslie was saying, reaching toward Dan's rifle.

"I'll take my chances," Steadman said. "I've got nothing to lose."

"You won't be able to let them go anyway," Dan said. "Just drop the gun and back away."

"I guess I'll just kill them and show you I mean what I say!" Steadman yelled.

"Dan! Please! Don't let him do it!" Leslie was nearly crazy with fear and concern. She took Dan's rifle and tried to pull it away from him.

Steadman started laughing. "Listen to her," he advised Dan. "She knows I mean it."

Leslie held the barrel of Dan's rifle firmly and Steadman decided he would take the opportunity to try to finish him then and there. He turned his pistol from Gus's head toward Dan and Gus yelled.

Dan released his rifle and Leslie stumbled backward with it. Dan jumped to the ground and rolled, just as Steadman fired. Steadman fired twice, missing Dan both times. He had cocked the

85

pistol for another shot when he stopped and turned to see five riders racing their horses down the hill from the canyon.

Dan was on his feet, but Steadman held the gun against Gus's head once again.

"They look like lawmen to me," Steadman said. "And it's your fault, Slayter." He pulled the trigger against Gus's head, but the chamber only snapped on cold steel. The gun was empty.

Steadman cursed and slammed the butt of the pistol into the top of Gus's head, sending him to the porch, unconscious. He turned to run but Dan was right behind him and tackled him viciously.

The deputies from Lovell rode into the yard and both Sally and Leslie were pointing up onto the hill, where Keith Larson and Steadman's horse hunters were riding their horses across the ridge to escape.

Steadman was yelling as Dan hauled him to his feet. Steadman swung hard, but Dan blocked the blow and slammed his fist into Steadman's mouth, driving him backward to the ground. Dazed, Steadman rolled over onto his stomach and pushed himself to his hands and knees, spitting blood and pieces of teeth from his mouth.

Leslie and Sally ran to the porch to take care of their parents. Sally went in for a cold cloth to put to Gus's forehead, while Leslie got her mother up and into her rocker.

Steadman shook his head and came to his feet, wobbly, then turned and tried to punch Dan once again. Dan sent a powerful blow with his fist into Steadman's midriff, doubling him over and sending him back down to the ground. Dan went to his saddlebags, took out a pair of handcuffs, and locked Steadman's hands behind him, leaving him to recover on the ground.

Dan looked out toward the ridge that led into the mountains above the ranch. Steadman's men were now gone into the canyon country, a good way ahead of the deputies. Dan knew he had the main horse hunter in Steadman, but wanted Keith Larson and the others to stand trial as well.

That would mean figuring a way to split forces with the men who had come up, since it didn't appear that Williams and the SWAT team were going to arrive anytime soon.

Dan thought about how he was going to be able to accomplish it all while he walked to the porch. There, Sally and Leslie were in a heated argument, while Sally tended to the headwound Steadman had given her father.

"What's the matter with you, Sally?" Leslie was asking her. "He would have killed our folks. You saw it with your own eyes. How could you ever have believed he cared about anything?"

Sally was nodding. Her face was flushed with anger, but tears were streaming down her face. "I know it," she said. "But I wanted more than just to stay on this dirty old place. Maybe it's good enough for you, but I want more."

"We don't need any more than what we've got here," Leslie came back. "You get down below and people are worse off the more they got. What's wrong with these mountains?"

"Nolan promised he could give me a good life

and we'd still have the mountains," Sally said. "I just ain't the kind of person who can live every day day doing the same things. I want more."

Leslie went into the house and returned with a glass of cold water for her mother. Sally changed the bandage on her father's head and noticed how silent he was. Sadie was rocking in her chair now, looking out over the country, with tears streaming down her face.

Steadman had crawled around the edge of the house and was sitting with his back against the wall. Dan walked around and Steadman spit at him. Dan wondered if there was anybody alive— including Sally—whom Steadman didn't want to spit at.

Then Dan looked out to the ridge again and saw that the deputies from Lovell were returning. They hadn't caught up to any of Steadman's men and that meant there was a lot of work ahead. No matter how the Wilkenses settled their family problems, there was going to be a lot of trouble for them before the horse hunters were all taken from their land.

NINE

The five deputies who had come up from Lovell now rode down from the ridge and into the ranch yard. The one in charge was an undersheriff from a nearby county named Chris Benson. He was older than Dan by a good ten years, and he looked Dan over carefully.

Benson had come ready to fight an army. He carried a rifle and a shotgun, plus two .44 Magnum pistols and bags filled with ammunition. His eyes were those of a man who wanted finally to have his chance to catch a criminal. He wanted to be a hero.

"I would have chased those men clear to hell and back," Benson said to Dan after introducing himself. "But I knew you had the main one down here already." He glanced over to where Steadman was still sitting in the shade with his back against the ranch house. "I figure we can get the others easy enough," he added.

Dan noticed that Benson hadn't bothered to introduce the men with him. The other four were younger than Dan and looked as if this was their first job of this sort. Unlike Benson, they had no inclinations to become heroes, and wished they were someplace else besides in deep canyon country chasing a group of men who killed lawmen just for the fun of it.

"A lot of our men are off fighting fire in the Wind River," one of the other men said to Dan, apologizing. "I guess the five of us will have to do."

Benson looked hard at the young lawman. "You take five good men and they can get just about anybody."

The younger lawman shrugged.

Benson turned back to Dan and looked him up and down again. "It's a good thing we showed up when we did," he said. "It seems we kept the others from coming down on you."

"How about Williams and the federal SWAT team?" Dan asked, ignoring Benson's blast of ego. "Are they coming?"

"As far as I know," Benson answered. "We've been on the trail for most of the morning and have heard little on our radio. I guess we can't pick up much in those canyons."

"We need them bad now," Dan said. "Worse than we did before."

Benson didn't seem to understand. "Why do we need them so bad? You've got Steadman."

"We've got Steadman," Dan said. "But I would like to get Keith Larson and all the rest of them as well. They'll come back here and try for the Wilkenses if they aren't taken into custody. We need to catch up to them before they formulate a plan to stir things up again."

"Some of us can take Steadman back down," Benson said. "Then the rest can stay and help you until the SWAT team arrives."

"I'd rather wait for the rest of the men to show up first," Dan said. "No use leaving without Steadman and all the others at once, if we can round them up. And it's not a good idea to try to take Steadman in without a lot of backup available."

Benson grunted. "I guess you want to be there when the press asks who got Steadman."

"I don't care about that," Dan said calmly. "I just care that when the press asks who got him that we've really got him. He's not behind bars yet and there're a number of horse hunters up here who don't want him going down and telling on them as well."

Benson grunted again. Dan watched the younger lawman who had spoken up before. He was just looking out over the country. The other three were listening intently, wondering what danger Benson was going to subject them to—possibly needlessly.

"It's not going to be easy to get Steadman down out of here," Dan said again. "We have to be careful."

"Maybe you're right," Benson conceded. "But what about the rest of them? Where do you think they're headed?"

"Not all of Steadman's men were with him," Dan explained. "It's my guess that half of them broke off and went up into the high country to find the stallion. Steadman has been obsessed with that horse."

"How do we handle it, then?" Benson asked.

"We've got Steadman," Dan said. "Let's just sit tight and see if the others with Steadman come back, or if they go up to join the others. We should know before very long, and that should give the SWAT team time to arrive."

Benson seemed impatient, as if he wanted to get Steadman onto his horse and start down the hill toward Lovell. Dan felt that Benson wanted it to be over now, that he wanted to get Steadman down through the steep canyon trails and into the flash of media cameras and television lights. It was a long way back through the rocks, and Dan wondered if Benson had thought about that.

Dan went over to where Steadman was now standing with his back against the house, glaring at him. Steadman watched Dan's approach, blood caked on his lips and in the cuts along his face.

"We're going to put you in the barn, Steadman," Dan said. "That way, respectable people won't have to look at you."

"I'll kill you, Slayter," Steadman hissed. "Just give me the chance, and I'll kill you."

"You had your chance," Dan told him. "Now you're going down and stand trial for a lot of things—including the death of my best friend. You had better say goodbye to these mountains, since you'll never see them again."

Steadman moved across the yard reluctantly. But he did keep moving, as he knew Dan Slayter needed little reason to start into him again. And already two of his front teeth were falling out.

Dan took him into the barn and secured the handcuffs that bound Steadman to a length of support beam that held the barn up. Steadman was not going to go anywhere and he knew it. But he was still confident that he was not in any real danger of going to jail.

As Dan was turning to leave, Steadman grunted and flicked out the two front teeth that were loose. He grinned at Dan through the bloody slot.

"Don't be so sure that you'll see me in front of a jury, Slayter. You haven't gotten me down through that canyon yet."

Dan came back out to where Benson and the others were talking about the situation. Benson had radioed down below and had learned that the SWAT team was going to be some time in getting up into the canyons. There had been trouble with one of the helicopters and some of the team members had gone to the wrong location.

Setbacks like that were not what Dan wanted at this time. Even though Steadman was stuck tight in the barn, Larson and the others were still on the loose. And the group that had gone up into the higher country after the stallion were likely waiting for the others to join them right now. And if they had the stallion trapped somewhere, they could move him out fast and there would be no way to stop them.

The longer Dan thought about it, the more he was convinced that he needed to get up into the high county and locate the stallion. It wouldn't matter if the rest of Steadman's men had already found the horse; what mattered was that they didn't take him anywhere. Dan reasoned that if he was up there, they wouldn't get the chance to move the stallion out of the mountains.

But he would need help in accomplishing what

he wanted. Benson could take Steadman down into Lovell if he wanted—when the SWAT team arrived—and that way he could spare a couple of the young deputies to go up into the high country.

Dan proposed the idea to Benson, while the other deputies listened.

"I would like to borrow a couple of your men and go up and make sure that stallion isn't herded out of the mountains," Dan began. "I'm worried that the stallion will be gone and there will be no reason for the others to stay in the area. We'll never find them all once they've left."

Benson agreed. He realized Dan was telling him that he was going to be taking Steadman down himself. He listened to Dan closely.

"When the SWAT team gets here," Dan added, "they can keep some of the men here to watch the ranch and send the rest up to help with Steadman's men. Then you can go out with Steadman in the helicopter and put him in the jail down in Lovell."

"That sounds like a good plan to me," Benson said. "When do you intend to leave for the high country?"

"Right away," Dan said. He was looking at the young deputy who had spoken up earlier, and another man right next to him.

Benson saw who Dan was looking at and introduced the young deputy as Clint Phillips. Phillips took Dan's hand, unable to conceal his excitement at being chosen to go up and save the stallion. He was of medium height and had dark features and a slight grin that now worked at his lips.

Ben Steiner was the other deputy. He was slightly built and blond, and shook Dan's hand with much more reserve.

"Glad to meet you both," Dan told them. "We've got some hard riding ahead. I hope you're both ready for it, in case you don't want this assignment."

Phillips and Steiner looked at each other. "We're ready for whatever comes," Phillips finally said, with his little smile.

"Good," Dan said. "I've got to get some things from the barn. Then we'll be ready."

Dan hurried to the barn, as the day was steadily passing. It would be late when they got into the high country. It didn't matter, though, as long as they got to the stallion ahead of Steadman's men.

Steadman was in the barn almost hanging from the handcuffs. He was out of breath from trying to pull them loose from the barn pole. His wrists were bleeding and he was frothing at the mouth. As soon as he heard Dan come in, he began screaming curses without even looking up.

Dan ignored him and set to finding the things he needed for the trip into the high country. Besides his bedroll, he took what he thought necessary to last as long as it took to save the stallion and bring the other horse hunters down to justice.

He piled his gear just outside the barn door and walked to his horse. Leslie and Sally had emerged from the house, where they had left their parents resting. While Sally talked to Benson and the deputies, Leslie started for the barn.

Dan was loading his gear on his horse when

Leslie came up to him.

"Are you going to leave?" she asked in a concerned voice.

"Just for a while," Dan said with a nod, throwing the saddle on the horse's back. "I'm taking two of the deputies into the high country to look for the stallion and the herd."

"I'm going with you," Leslie said.

"No, stay here," Dan ordered. "You might need to help Benson and the rest of his deputies if Keith Larson shows up with the other horse hunters while I'm gone."

"You said there was going to be a bunch of men in a helicopter coming," she said. "Won't they be safe?"

Dan thought about it. With Benson and two deputies, and Sally, there shouldn't be any problem. And when the SWAT team arrived, there would be a lot of men to watch the ranch. As far as protection for Gus and Sadie was concerned, he wasn't worried. But how could he explain it to them if something happened to Leslie?

"You can't leave without me," Leslie told Dan emphatically. "I don't care what you say, I'm going up there with you."

"What makes you think it's worth risking your life over?"

"I want this over with," she replied. "I've had enough of Steadman and his gang."

"It's my job to get Steadman's gang," Dan reminded her. "I wouldn't like it if something happened to you. It's also my job to see to it that doesn't happen."

"You don't know where the stallion goes up there," Leslie said. "I do. And I know where the box canyon is that they want to catch him in, the same one they catch all the wild mustangs in."

Dan looked at her with interest. "Couldn't you just tell me how to get there? I mean it—I don't want you to risk your life going up there with us."

"If you don't know those mountains, you'll have a hard time," she said. "I need to guide you through that country up there."

Without waiting to hear anything else from Dan, Leslie immediately went into the corral and caught her horse. She quickly put on a bridle and saddle and led the horse past Dan, who was climbing into the saddle.

"I'm going into the house to pack some things, as we will likely be staying out," she said. "You leave without me and I'll just have to catch up somehow." She looked at Dan, waiting for his response.

Dan tried to hide his grin. Leslie was insistent in a lot of ways, and he knew she meant what she had just said.

"We'll wait for you," he said. "Just hurry."

Keith Larson had the men sitting around him at the edge of Devil Canyon. They now had major problems of the kind that needed immediate attention.

One was that Nolan Steadman was now in custody and could implicate all of them in the death of Chuck Farley and the attempted theft of the BLM wild mustangs. They would all have their names handed to someone looking to hunt them down, no matter what state they tried to hide in.

And the wild stallion was the second big concern. Claude Mosely was up there with the rest of the men waiting for Steadman to come up and say that Dan Slayter was dead and their only problem was to get the stallion out of the mountains and retreat somewhere to let the stallion sire bucking horses.

But the meeting with Claude Mosely could not take place until they got Steadman back. Larson had led the men up through the canyon into the higher country, breaking off their trail where it mixed with the tracks of the wild horses. He didn't know if anyone would be behind them, tracking them, but he didn't want to take any chances.

After taking the men in a circle through the canyon, Larson discussed the possibility of going back down to the Wilkens ranch. His main concern was Nolan Steadman.

"We got to get him away from them lawmen," one of the men suggested.

"We don't want him down there telling who all he had in his gang," another horse hunter put in.

Larson nodded. He wanted to say something in the worst way—that they should think of it from the standpoint that Steadman shouldn't get to the bottom—period. But he was afraid if he brought up that they should get rid of Steadman at the same time they took care of the lawmen, somebody might take offense.

It wasn't so much that all the men thought

highly of Steadman. Larson was well aware that some of the men were on the verge of quitting, just because he was so unpredictable. No one knew from day to day what his mood was going to be or what he might get angry about. It was getting harder and harder to put up with.

And Larson realized as well that if the men knew what had really happened to the two Steadman had shot in his house, they would certainly think hard about staying around. But after today, with all of them taking part in shooting at Dan Slayter, everyone had to work together until everything was resolved.

"The way I see it," Larson told the group, "I don't want to miss out on all the time I've put into catching horses and selling them—especially that stallion. If Steadman is taken to trial, that will all go down the drain. And he could take us all under with him."

The men voiced agreement. To a man they understood that Steadman could not go to trial, under any circumstances. They had to get him back from the custody of the lawmen. One way or another, he couldn't get down off the mountain.

More discussion was held and they all agreed to send two riders up into the high country to find Claude Mosely and the other half of the group, to apprise them of what had happened. They would have to put off catching the stallion until Steadman was back with them. Meanwhile, the rest, under Keith Larson, would go back down to the Wilkens ranch and get Steadman away from the lawmen.

As they broke camp and prepared for the late

evening ride down to the Wilkens ranch, Larson contemplated how hard it would be to get Steadman away from the lawmen. Dan Slayter was turning out to be much more than a handful. There was not much chance that he could be fooled by any conventional means.

Larson had watched from the hill while Steadman had stood on the porch, holding the gun against the old man's head. If Slayter had been given an inch to shoot through, he would have killed Steadman on the spot. Larson had thought at the time how foolish Steadman had been to go down there alone and to think he could make Slayter do what he wanted. "If all of you come," Steadman had argued, "then Slayter will just shoot half of you and I won't get a chance at him."

Now Larson wished he hadn't listened to Steadman and had just ridden down the hill with the rest of the men. Some of them might have been killed, but at least they wouldn't be worried now about all of them going to jail.

As Larson led the men along a trail that would take them back down to the Wilkens ranch, he wondered what they would face. He didn't know exactly how they were going to get past Slayter and the others to Steadman, but he knew they had to. One way or another, they had to get Steadman back.

TEN

Sally paced the porch outside the kitchen door and looked often into the sky, where a helicopter filled with men was supposed to descend to provide them safety and take Nolan Steadman down to Lovell. But the sky was empty, and as time continued to pass, she became more and more concerned.

Almost three hours had passed since Dan Slayter and Leslie had left for the high country with the two young deputies. Her parents were in their rocking chairs, seemingly in a daze. Periodically, one or both of them would retreat into the house to lie down and try to rest away their shock.

Nolan Steadman had been to the ranch many times before, and he had always shown that he was a killer. In fact, Gus had said often that he thought Steadman hated him for some reason. But the actual act of having a gun put to your head is much more than just thinking it could happen.

Now Sally was concerned that Keith Larson and the others might return at any time to try to get Steadman back. She worried that Larson was aware that Dan Slayter was no longer at the ranch and that he was rubbing his hands together in anticipation of swooping down on those who were left.

There had been no shots from the higher country above the ranch and Sally felt somehow that Larson and the others had avoided contact with Dan and her sister, with the two young deputies. She realized that if the helicopter didn't show up soon, there would be more trouble, and worse than before.

While she had been pacing the porch, Sally had been watching Chris Benson pacing the ranch yard. Periodically, he would go into the barn and check on Steadman, then return outside to wander the corrals and kick dirt with his boots.

Finally, he called his deputies from where they lounged in the shade, and told them to saddle their horses. Sally watched with curiosity and concern as he went into the barn and brought Steadman out. Shortly, he was leading Steadman to his horse.

Sally walked over to where he was preparing to leave.

"What are you doing?" she asked Benson.

Benson looked at her quickly and began tying things on his saddle.

"I can't wait any longer for the SWAT team," he finally told her. "I'm going to take Steadman down to Lovell."

"You can't do that," Sally blurted. "Not on your own, not and just leave us here alone."

"I'm in charge here," Benson came back. "I have

to take this man down to stand trial."

Sally looked at Steadman, who was grinning, the gap in his teeth showing where Dan Slayter had punched him. She wondered how she could ever have been taken in by this man. She turned back to Benson.

"What are we going to do here by ourselves?" Sally asked him again. "My folks are in real danger if the rest of the horse hunters come back here."

"I have to get this man down to justice," Benson insisted, pointing to Steadman. "That's the first priority."

"And if we all die in the meantime?"

Benson climbed on his horse and looked at Sally a long moment. Finally, he said, "Maybe the SWAT team will make it up here." Then he turned his horse and led the way for the column of riders.

Benson was in the lead, with a deputy right behind him. Steadman was in the middle and the other two deputies followed him, in single file. Just before they got out of the yard, Steadman turned in the saddle and called back to Sally.

"See you before long."

Dan led the small posse—the two deputies and Leslie—up the steepening trails toward the upper reaches of the Bighorn Mountains. Larson and the horse hunters with him had left a trail broad enough to follow for a good distance. Though it was rocky in places, the ground was dry and the hoofprints could be read easily.

Dan knew, however, that the higher they rode,

the harder it was going to be to follow them—especially now that they were getting into the area where the mustangs were ranging. Leslie told Dan that these upper reaches were where they would find the stallion.

She was right. They began to find numerous horse tracks going everywhere, and they mixed with the trail of the horse hunters, making it impossible to know which direction Larson had taken his men.

Even though Larson and the others had shod horses, there were so many fresh tracks going so many directions that it made following a trail impossible.

And the country here was making Dan nervous. Ambushes could be planned easily by somebody who knew the lay of the land. The canyons were deeper and more narrow here, with long drops into nothing. Rock formations rose high above the trails and any number of men could hide in just a little space.

Besides the rocks, there was a lot of other cover as well. There was much more timber now, tightly packed and taller in height. The dusty stretches of rabbitbrush and big sagebrush had changed into grass meadows and woody draws. The hills had more vegetation as the altitude increased and the annual precipitation was greater.

Leslie took Dan and the two young deputies out of the canyon and they rode along the less traveled trails that skirted the rims. Dan had pretty much given up on being able to track Larson and the horse hunters any farther, so there was no need to worry about them at the present time. Right now, he was worried about keeping all of them alive.

The trails along the rims were harder to negotiate and their pace dropped off considerably. But they would not have to worry about an ambush. Now the most important thing was finding the stallion and his herd, and moving them back down to the wild horse range and away from the horse hunters.

As late afternoon wore on, Dan grew more concerned about the backup help that was supposed to arrive. Phillips and Steiner had heard nothing on their radios and there had been no sign of a helicopter. Dan finally came to the conclusion that the SWAT team was not going to make it at all, at least before the next morning.

He wondered now if Larson and the others had circled back around to make a raid on the ranch and get Steadman back. It was beginning to look more and more as if Larson had led them up high and then made a circle back, mixing his trail with that of the mustangs.

Dan was certain now that Larson and the others would likely try to get Steadman back, but he could only hope that the undersheriff, Chris Benson, used his deputies to their fullest capacity to hold Larson off.

But something told him that Benson would not be able to hold on to Steadman.

The more he thought about it, the more he was certain that Benson would have a hard time. The older lawman was too bitter to think rationally in times of stress, and he would want to prove himself.

If only the SWAT team would arrive, Dan

thought to himself. But that wasn't going to happen, and he knew there was going to be trouble down at the Wilkens ranch.

Sally was combing burrs out of her horse's coat when she heard the riders coming. She looked up along the ridge behind the barn, to see that whoever had come was now taking position in the trees up there—the same place Steadman had taken them just before dawn to ambush Dan Slayter.

She knew instinctively that it was Keith Larson —that he had come back for Steadman. And she knew he could easily see that Steadman was not there, nor was Dan Slayter and the other lawmen. Larson would see easily that hers was now the only horse in the corral.

Sally dropped the currycomb and ran from the corral toward the house. Her parents were on the porch in their rockers and had already seen Larson and the others. They were up from their chairs, calling to Sally and getting ready to go inside the house to cover.

She was very afraid now, as she could hear Larson and the others yelling as they rode down off the ridge. They had nothing to fear now, and they might destroy everything for the fun of it.

Sally gathered up all the nerve she could and waited for them on the porch as they rode to a stop in the yard. She knew she was helpless to do anything to stop them from whatever they wished to do, but she would tell them the lawmen were all gone and Steadman was with them on their way down to Lovell.

"No one is here but my folks and myself," she told Larson when he asked.

"I can see that," Larson said, looking around. "There's no place to hide horses near here, not and have them up where they could get stolen."

"So, there's no reason for you to stay here," Sally said.

Larson got down from his horse. "Maybe. Maybe not. Did Slayter take Steadman down?"

Sally thought for a moment before she answered. She knew Larson would be a lot more worried if Slayter had taken Steadman than under the real circumstances.

"All I know is, they all left," she finally said. "Everybody split up and left."

"Where's your sister?" Larson asked. He was walking toward the house, looking all around again.

"She went along."

"Went along with who?"

"Dan Slayter."

Larson grunted. "Doesn't Slayter know the way down out of here?" He thought a moment, then added, "Or doesn't he know the high country as well as your sister? Did she take him up into the mountains?"

"I told you, they all left," Sally said. "I didn't pay any attention to who went where."

"No, I'll bet you didn't," Larson said. He stopped in front of her and she could see the distrust in his eyes. "I'm going inside," he said, and pushed past her.

"What do you want in there?" Sally asked him, following.

"I just want to make sure Slayter didn't tie Nolan up in here and leave him, so he could get him when he came back down."

Sally stood with her parents for a time while Larson searched the house. While he looked, he examined items and put some money he found on a dresser into his pocket.

"Steadman is not in here," Sally said firmly. "Please, just leave."

Larson ignored her pleas to stop looking through the house. He was opening all the closet doors he could find and every so often he would turn and scowl at her and her parents.

"This place have a cellar?" he asked.

Sally took him out and around to the side of the house, where a wooden stairway led down into a damp cellar. Larson peered inside the small space and, finally content that Steadman was not tied and gagged and stashed somewhere, decided to go back to his horse.

He stood beside the horse, his arm resting across the pommel, and looked up at the ridge above the ranch.

"Those lawmen decided to take Nolan down by themselves, did they?" he asked. He turned to Sally and smiled. "Some of them must have gone with your sister and Slayter. I'd bet there's only three or four of them with Nolan—ain't that right?"

Sally shrugged.

Larson laughed. "Yeah, I'll bet that's right."

He looked up onto the ridge again and then took a length of rope from his saddle and came back to Sally.

"Well, I know one thing for sure—you're going with us," he said. "That should make Nolan pretty happy, don't you think?"

"I'm going to stay here and take care of my folks," Sally said. "They're not doing well at all, not after this morning."

"That's a shame," Larson said. "But they'll have to get along without you. Now, saddle your horse and let's go. We haven't got a lot of time."

"I'm not going with you," Sally said firmly.

Larson snorted, with the other men. "Either you come peaceful, or I'll hogtie you on your horse. Which do you want?"

Sally realized she had no choice. She finally decided she would have to do what she was told, but succeeded in getting Larson to allow her to tell her folks what was happening.

Larson walked up beside her. "I'd better go back in with you," he said. "I don't want that old couple to think about shooting us, or something."

"Just wait on the porch, would you?" Sally asked. "They aren't going to try and stop you. Nolan almost killed them this morning."

"Are you still sweet on him?" Larson asked.

"I'm not sweet on anybody," Sally answered.

She went inside the house and found her father standing at the broken kitchen window, listening. Her mother was just a little way behind him.

"I'm sorry," Sally said. "They're forcing me to go with them."

109

Gus nodded. "Just don't do anything foolish, girl. We want you to come back to us."

Sally hugged both her parents. Tears trailed from her mother's eyes and hers as well.

"Hurry up!" Larson yelled from the porch.

"I'll be back soon," Sally promised as she started out toward the porch. "I'll be back as soon as I can."

"Maybe those other lawmen will come," her mother said.

"Maybe," Sally said with a nod. "But that won't help us now."

ELEVEN

Larson led the men along the upper reaches of Cottonwood Canyon to where they could look down through the rocks to the trail below. They had made good time and now Larson was hoping they had gotten far enough ahead of the lawmen to set up an ambush.

Sally rode with them, in silence for the most part. She answered questions only when forced. She knew she had a lot of information that Larson would like to hear—that would help him find Steadman and the lawmen taking him down the canyon. But she wasn't about to tell him any more than she had to, especially after what had happened that morning.

For some time she had had it in the back of her head that Nolan Steadman was using her, that he didn't care about building a career as a rodeo queen for her. But she didn't want to admit it to herself, and she certainly didn't want to think her sister, Leslie, was telling her the truth.

She wanted to think that Leslie was jealous, that Leslie wished *she* was going to be a rodeo queen.

Leslie had told her often to stop and think what she was doing—that Nolan Steadman was bad and only wanted her for one thing. There was no way, according to Leslie, that Nolan Steadman could have any aboveboard ties with anybody.

Sally knew there had been times when she wanted to break away from Steadman. But he had control of her some way then. He had control then, but certainly not now. What he had done to her parents was unforgivable.

She could still see them in her mind: terrorized and wondering if Steadman was going to kill them all. She could see her mother, stumbling and dazed after Steadman's blow. And her father, thinking his life had finally come to an end.

Now Sally was mad at herself. There was no excuse for what had happened and she had been a part of it. She had been with Steadman when they had taken position in the trees and had tried to gun down Dan Slayter. She had even tried to help by riding out to where her sister had taken position, and working to keep her from using her own rifle.

Sally thought also that there was something about herself that she was going to have to face from now on and live with—something that was real, but did not make her any less a person. And that was the problem with her mind that she had suffered since falling off the horse at a young age.

She was well aware that because of the fall, she suffered from a nervous disorder that brought feelings of deep insecurity to her. She knew that was what had blinded her to the real Nolan Steadman in the first place. When he had told her how beautiful she was and how he could make everybody in the world appreciate that beauty, he was only feeding on her insecurities.

And he had fed upon them for a long time. She felt she should have been able to see long ago that Steadman only wanted her for the times he took her to bed and nothing more. He had never once taken her down off the mountain to a rodeo, or to introduce her to people who could make her a rodeo queen. Never once did he ever do any of what he had promised her. It was always next time, next time he would take her with him.

Sally was determined now that there would be no next time. Though Keith Larson had her with them, she wouldn't tell them anything about what she knew concerning the lawmen and their attempt to get Steadman down to Lovell. Larson would have to learn everything on his own. And she hoped he failed.

But Larson had an arrogant air about him and didn't seem to care how much he learned from her. He seemed to know for sure now that Dan Slayter was headed for the high country and not taking Steadman down to stand trial. This would make it a lot easier to get Steadman back, as the lawmen with Steadman really had no idea there was anyone on their trail.

Larson hurried them along now, looking into the sky every few minutes. She knew Larson's intention was to ambush the lawmen as soon as possible, as the day was fast wearing into evening. They couldn't afford to try the ambush in the dark and risk not making it work.

Larson was complaining as they rode that they weren't going to get to what he called the "crook in the trail" before the lawmen and Steadman passed it. But soon Larson and the rest with him smiled to themselves. They had won the race. Just a way up the trial were five riders, with Nolan Steadman in the middle of them.

Larson looked through binoculars and could see that Steadman was handcuffed. He was looking up through the rocks and by the expression on his face, he had about given up on anybody coming to get him away from the lawmen.

Larson thought to himself that it wouldn't take much now to get Steadman free, if they placed their shots just right. None of the lawmen seemed too concerned about what was going on around them and the one in the lead seemed to be proud of himself, sitting up straight on his horse.

Near the top of a trail that led down into the canyon, Larson stopped and got down from his horse. He took a length of rope from his saddle and pulled Sally down from her horse.

"Let's find a tree and tie you to it," he told her. "You'll just be in the way down there in the canyon."

Sally knew there was little she could do about it, and allowed Larson to tie her securely to a tree and stuff a bandana into her mouth. He certainly didn't want her yelling any warnings to the lawmen.

Larson took one last look at Sally and wished to himself that she was his. He got up on his horse and started with the others down the trail into the canyon, thinking that Steadman didn't appreciate what he had in the woman. In fact, he didn't appreciate anything he had at all.

Behind the curve in the trail, Larson and the others took position to await the lawmen. The canyon was finally beginning to cool down from the midday sun and it seemed natural to assume that the lawmen would be eager to get down below and would be riding only half-alert.

Finally, the lawmen arrived. Larson had placed himself where he could get the lead man, the one who was so proud of himself, and then help the others with the rest of them. Their only real concern was in hitting Steadman.

Larson wasn't entirely opposed to putting Steadman away with the others. But he realized if Steadman was killed, that would make it hard to profit even a little from all this trouble. Steadman had all the contacts through which to sell rodeo stock and he had carefully kept them to himself over the years.

So, in fact, it was necessary to keep Steadman alive. There was no one in the group who thought for a moment that Steadman would be grateful to any of them for being delivered from the mess he had gotten himself into, but the feel of money could erase the lack of appreciation.

While Keith Larson and the others prepared their ambush, Chris Benson led the lawmen down the trail toward the curve that went around a large column of rocks. They had faith in him, and though some of them had thought leaving with Steadman might not be a good idea, they still backed him and were anxious to get down out of the canyon.

Benson felt he had made the right decision in leaving with Steadman and hoping to get him down the canyon and into jail. He knew Dan Slayter likely wouldn't approve when he got back from the Bighorns. But by then it wouldn't matter; Steadman would be behind bars.

Benson thought he could certainly justify his actions by his concern over the other horse hunters possibly coming back to the ranch. He didn't think he had enough men to hold off an all-out attack and since the SWAT team hadn't been able to get organized and arrive, he felt he was obligated to see to it that Steadman went down the canyon to justice.

A lot of it had to do with his determination to be recognized. For as long as he had been in law enforcement, he had never won a county sheriff election, though he had run four different times. That was too many to have lost and be able to save face.

Benson was certain that he had been a much better lawman than a lot of those younger guys who were now in office in different parts of Montana and Wyoming. This young Dan Slayter was a good case in point: he couldn't be thirty years old and he was working on a case that wasn't even in his own state.

No matter how he looked at it Chris Benson couldn't get himself to believe that Dan Slayter was as good as all that. He had to be something, though, to have survived the onslaught of Steadman and his horse hunters not just once, but twice already.

He couldn't know how it had been the day when Chuck Farley was killed; but he did know the day they came up out of the canyon and into the Wilkens ranch yard: Dan Slayter was a hair's breadth away from either dying or putting Nolan Steadman away forever.

Benson now felt that bringing Steadman down would give him the notoriety he needed to gain a county sheriff's job himself, possibly. He had wanted an assignment like this for a long, long time, but he had never gotten one. With a lot of men fighting fires and other problems around the state and region, he was getting his first chance to prove that he should be considered a top lawman.

Benson was thinking about all of this as he led Steadman and the other deputies around the curve in the trail. A few hours' time would bring them relief and a waving, shouting crowd of admiring people.

Then something flashed in the rocks just above and ahead of him—something bright, like the glint of sunshine off metal.

He realized too late that it was a rifle barrel that had caught his eye. Just as soon as the flash of steel registered in his brain, there was a flash of a different sort and Benson felt a searing pain in his lower chest.

He doubled over and fell sideways from the bolting horse as another bullet tore into the top of his shoulder. He could hear Steadman and his deputies yelling behind him. But it was a vague and hazy sort of acknowledgement, as if everything was far away and he was drifting somewhere, almost up into the air.

His body kept feeling lighter and the pain seemed almost to go away. Finally, he drifted into deep black.

Upon the first shots, Steadman had watched Benson fall and was jumping off his own horse. The deputy just ahead of him was screaming and holding his hands in front of him as bullet after bullet slammed into him.

Steadman, now on the ground, ran awkwardly to get out of the line of fire and to make better targets of the two deputies still in the saddle behind him.

Then one of them fired at him and the bullet tore the top of his ear off, sending him to the ground, dazed. Another bullet tore into the rocks near his stomach, and then he turned to gather his strength and rise. At that moment, he saw another rifle aimed at him.

But the rifle fell from the hands of the young deputy as a shot from one of his men entered the lawman's cheek and tore out the side of his face. The rifle dropped from the deputy's hands and he grabbed the saddlehorn by instinct.

Larson and the other horse hunters were now out of the rocks and were surrounding the last deputy, who sat in the saddle at an awkward angle, with his face a mess. He took more bullets, which struck him everywhere, and died before he tumbled from the saddle.

Steadman came to his knees and finally to his

feet. Benson and the other deputies were all lying in the rocks bleeding, so he saw no reason to be concerned about them. But his own face was covered with blood and he didn't know yet whether or not he was going to die.

Finally, he realized he had lost the top of his right ear. He cursed. He stood in the trail and watched Larson turn over Benson's body to get at the handcuff key. Then they all came over to him through the haze of dust and gunsmoke, and Larson unlocked the handcuffs.

"You're a mess," Larson told him. "But you ain't dead."

Steadman shook his head and held his hand to his bleeding ear.

"It's about time you got here," Steadman told Larson. "I thought you'd all left me to go to jail down below."

Larson grunted. "It's about time you decided you owe somebody else for a change, instead of them always owing you."

Steadman stared at Larson, unable to believe the backtalk he had just heard. The others were looking on, without speaking. Larson finally told them to get their horses and get ready to move out.

"What you tryin' to tell me, Larson?" Steadman asked, when the others were out of earshot.

"I want a little more respect, Steadman," Larson said flatly. "We rode hard to get you out of this mess and all you do is bellyache. It seems to me you got yourself into all this by wanting to take care of Slayter all by yourself."

"Like I told you," Steadman came back, "a

whole bunch of men would just have botched it up worse."

"You couldn't have botched it up much worse," Larson said with a grunt. "And with all of us to back you, we would have made sure Slayter was dead."

"Slayter would have shot half of you, and you know it," Steadman argued.

"Not when you were holding the gun on the old man," Larson came back. "He didn't want the old man to die, but he knew you couldn't just kill him and then make it out of there on your own."

Steadman rubbed his wrists to get the circulation back and thought about Larson's boldness. He might be right about the way the Slayter situation was handled, but that was a thing of the past and they still had him to contend with. There was no good bickering when they had a job to do.

"Well, next time I'll do it different," Steadman finally said.

Larson was surprised to hear Steadman admit to being wrong, but he had more to say anyway.

"You're just lucky these lawmen wanted to take you down and not wait for more men to show up," he added. "And it's a good thing Slayter wasn't here. We wouldn't have had such an easy time of it."

"You heard me, Larson," Steadman suddenly blurted. "We'll all have to work together to get Slayter. So let's drop it and get out of here."

The other men were now sacking guns and ammunition and other valuables from the fallen deputies. Steadman found a canteen on one of the horses and began to wash the blood off his head and neck. His ear was tender and beginning to swell a great deal, and he cursed again.

"We brought Sally along with us," Larson told Steadman. "She won't want to kiss you now, not with that ear of yours the way it is."

"What's all the sudden humor?" Steadman asked Larson. "All at once you're some kind of clown."

"Just havin' some fun," Larson said. "Ain't you glad we brought Sally back to you?"

"Yeah, I'm glad. Where is she?"

"We left her up above, where she wouldn't be in on the shooting. She's tied up."

"She'd better not have gotten away," Steadman warned. "If Slayter came along, he'd find her."

"Slayter went to the high country to look for the stallion," Larson informed Steadman. "I found that out from her back at the ranch. He's not coming down this way. I'd bet he thinks these lawmen still got you tied up in the barn."

"By rights they should have," Steadman said, smiling for the first time since telling Sally he'd see her before long. Then he pointed to the fallen Chris Benson. "That lawman there wanted to be a hero. I guess he's just another dead man now."

"We've got to move if we aim to get to that stallion and keep Slayter from running him back down off the mountain," Larson suggested. "It's lucky we found you when we did, with it getting late like it is."

Steadman nodded. Another hour and the sun would be close to setting. It had been a close call at that. And now there was the matter of Dan Slayter and where he was, and if he had found the stallion yet. Once that stallion was back down on the wild horse range, it would be nearly impossible to get him out again.

As they mounted up, Steadman tried to ignore the pain in his ear. He wondered if Claude Mosely and the other half of the gang had located the stallion and if they could hold off Dan Slayter when he found them. If Mosely and the others could just slow them up, it would be enough time to get there and, he hoped, end Slayter's trouble-making ways forever.

TWELVE

Steadman ordered the men to gather the horses that had belonged to the lawmen and trail them behind. Larson suggested they put the bodies of the lawmen over the horses and take them into the upper canyon country to get rid of them. Steadman conceded that the idea was good and that it might make him feel better about losing part of his ear if he could see their bodies growing stiff on the backs of their horses.

Larson was concerned less about Steadman's morbid sense of retribution than he was about reaching the herd of mustangs before Dan Slayter. It didn't matter that Claude Mosely was up there with half the men; Dan Slayter could account for a lot of odds, and Mosely had yet to see what Slayter could do in a shootout.

But it was too late in the day to think about getting up into the high country. They would likely pick up Sally from where she was tied and ride a little farther, then make camp and get an early start. No use trying to outdo Slayter in the dark.

But when they got back to where Sally had been tied, Larson suddenly got a cramped feeling in his stomach. He looked around and saw there was nobody tied to the tree. Sally Wilkens had somehow worked herself loose.

At least that was his first thought.

"I know I tied her right here," Larson said as Steadman cursed at him. He looked to the other men and they agreed.

"How could you let that happen?" Steadman asked Larson and the group as a whole. "Well?"

One of the men, who had been looking around, spoke up. "It looks to me like there's been some horses over close to where she was tied. There wasn't none of us rode over there, I know. We all just watched Keith tie her up."

The others concurred. It appeared that Sally had not gotten free by herself.

"Maybe someone did find her," Larson offered. "But who could that have been?"

They inspected the tree where Sally had been tied and found where the rope had been cut cleanly. But there was no way to know who had cut the rope or how many of them had come for her.

"That damn sheriff," Larson finally said.

"It couldn't have been Slayter," Steadman surmised. "Otherwise, he would have been after us before now. He wouldn't just take her and run off. He'd have been shootin' at us for sure."

"Then who?" Larson asked again.

Steadman looked hard at Larson and then back up the trail from the ranch. "Do you suppose that old man got brave?" he asked. "Maybe we ought to ride to the Wilkens ranch and see."

Sally rode on the horse her father had brought for her. Sadie was riding behind Sally, content to be in the saddle again, even if it meant going for a dangerous ride. She was getting up in years and only went for leisurely rides on occasion. But she realized she might never get to ride over her ranch again if she didn't help stop Nolan Steadman and his gang of horse hunters.

Sally rode between her mother and father, glad for their courage, yet worried about what could happen to them. But she believed what her father had told her when he had been cutting her free: "If I'm to die, I don't aim to be no coward when I go out."

Gus talked now as they rode, becoming more certain of himself now that they had succeeded in getting one of their daughters back with them. He rode as if he had had to fight for his land some time before, and Sally heard a story that made her sit up in the saddle in surprise.

"There was some drygulchers came down on us the year you and your sister were born," he began. "Your ma and I took it upon ourselves to drive them off. After that, we figured we'd come too close to killin' somebody and swore we'd never go to fightin' with guns again."

"But sometimes a person has to go back on what they think and do what's right," Sadie put in.

"Why didn't you tell Leslie and me about this before?" Sally asked.

"Didn't see the need," Gus answered. "We didn't want to bring up what wasn't good."

Sadie agreed with him, and then said something that made Sally certain her mother had been listening to Dan Slayter that first night on the porch, even though she had been pretending not to.

"It's time we stopped letting things go Steadman's way," she had said. "There's some men that ain't got no good in them a-tall. All he does is kill people."

Gus was riding with his Sharps rifle across the pommel of his saddle. He looked out into the deepening twilight and smiled.

"I wished we'd have done this two years ago," he said. "Then we wouldn't have had to put up with all this from Steadman. We'd either be dead or free, one or the other. I aim to stay free or die."

Sally was proud of what her parents had just done for her, though she knew this was just the beginning of a ride through hell for them. They weren't used to hard riding, but it would be necessary to stay ahead of Steadman and the others—and thus stay alive.

It was important now that they reach Dan Slayter and Leslie as quickly as possible. There was no sense in going back to the ranch; Steadman would just storm it and they wouldn't have a chance.

"We brought some clothes and whatever we'll need to make it," Gus told Sally as they discussed it. "We'll just take things as they come."

They rode at a good pace up into the high

canyon country. The sun was definitely on their side, and Sally tried to calm herself as she helped her father select a spot to make camp. The canyons were far too treacherous to try ascending at night, and they would have to be content with an early start when the sun came again.

"There's a box canyon up here somewhere that they use to trap the horses," Leslie was telling Dan as they rode. "I've never been to it, but I know generally where it's located. That's where we have to be if we want to save the stallion."

Dan was looking far across a broad canyon to where a herd of horses grazed along the rim. The big black was moving now, his head held high, his tail raised behind him. He was watching something across the far side of them, away from Dan and the others, so that they couldn't see what the stallion had spotted.

"Claude Mosely," Clint Phillips spoke up. "I'd bet good money on it."

"You might be right," Dan said. "But we don't want to be here if it is Claude Mosely."

Dan had learned from Clint that the man leading the other half of Steadman's gang was a wanted fugitive. Clint and the other, quieter, deputy, Ben Steiner, had told Dan a lot about the other men in Steadman's gang, as the sheriff's office in Lovell had been gathering information on the men running the canyons above Bighorn Lake.

Mosely was a hardcase from Oklahoma, wanted

in that state for murder and stock-rustling. He was an expert at moving horses and cattle long distances in a short period of time, then selling them and getting away with the money. During his last job in Oklahoma, a stock inspector had caught him loading race horses into a trailer and Mosely had shot him on the spot.

According to the information Clint Phillips had, Mosely had joined Steadman's gang to speed up the process of getting the black stallion and moving him out of the area quickly. Once he got the black into the box canyon, they would catch him and be gone in little time.

Dan glassed the far side of the canyon once again and saw that the stallion was watching something now that was not far away from their position. The stallion had moved his herd down the rim a way, indicating to Dan that who—or whatever—the stallion had been watching was now circling around from above and coming in their direction.

"I don't like this," Dan announced. "We'd better be watching closely as we ride."

The sun was now falling rapidly in the west and Dan listened to Leslie as she told of a place where they could take cover and camp for the night. She was pointing up toward the hills above them, to a high, timbered knoll, where a formation of dark clouds was shooting lightning down into the trees.

Evening thundershowers came and went quickly in this country. Water could come in a deluge and the sun be out in a matter of minutes, while the trees dripped water for hours.

The high hill would be a perfect spot to camp. They needed to be able to see for a distance, yet be concealed and not be spotted easily by Claude Mosely and the other half of Nolan Steadman's horse hunters. Where they were now, on a trail that led along an open ledge, someone could spot them easily.

Or maybe they already had.

As they got ready to ride toward the high hill, Clint Phillips called for them to hold up and got down from his horse. He checked his horse's left front foot and found the shoe was loose. He did what he could to pound the loose nails down with a rock, but it wasn't going to be sufficient to keep the shoe on for very much longer.

"I don't think I'll be much good to you with a lame horse," Clint said to Dan. "I'm sorry."

Dan got off his horse and looked at the loose shoe. Clint was right; there was a problem. It would be impossible for a lame horse to travel through the rocky country for very long without being immobilized completely.

They were talking about what to do when they suddenly heard shots coming from below. In the still mountain air, the gunfire carried plainly, and it was obvious that someone was doing a lot of shooting in the canyons below them.

Leslie immediately worried about Sally and her folks.

"Do you suppose Larson went back to the ranch to get Steadman?" Sally asked.

"That's very possible," Dan said. "But it sounds to me like the shooting is a lot lower than where your ranch is located."

Leslie tried to locate the gunfire by listening closely. Dan had his binoculars trained far down, but there was no way of seeing anything in the lengthening evening shadows.

Leslie thought finally that she had an idea where the shooting was taking place.

"It sounds to me like it's down in the middle of Cottonwood Canyon, below the ranch," Leslie said. "What do you think that means?"

Dan turned to Clint Phillips and Ben Steiner, who were both watching him closely. They all realized now that Chris Benson had left the ranch and had tried to take Steadman down to Lovell.

"I don't know for sure," Dan finally said to Leslie, "but I'm afraid Steadman is no longer at the ranch, and possibly Keith Larson and the others ambushed him and the deputies. If that's the case, there's not much hope for any of them."

The gunfire below stopped abruptly and the still air became peaceful once again. A feeling settled over Dan and Leslie and the two young deputies, a feeling of certain loss and tragedy.

Both Clint Phillips and Ben Steiner were sickened. They had been close friends with the other deputies, and they realized they were likely both dead now, victims of Steadman's men and Chris Benson's quest for glory.

Everyone was quiet. Clint Phillips dabbed at his eyes and looked into the distance. A couple of big black ravens flew overhead on their way to roost, cawing as they skimmed the treetops. A light breeze rustled the pines and the three finally broke their silence.

It was Clint Phillips who pointed to a trail just above them.

"It's Claude Mosely and the bunch with him,"

he said, his voice trembling. "They've spotted us."

The lightning storm had reached farther down off the hill now, and thunder was rolling right above them. Dan turned to see Claude Mosely and the horse hunters with him getting down off their horses. They pulled rifles from scabbards on their saddles and dropped to their knees to shoot.

"Leave your horse, Clint!" Dan yelled. "Get on behind me. Quick!"

Clint scrambled up behind Dan and Dan's horse lurched ahead, just as the first shots from Claude Mosely and the others echoed through the canyon. Clint yelled as a bullet creased the top of his shoulder, a bullet Dan knew had been meant for him.

More gunfire followed as Dan led Leslie and the other deputy off the lookout point and toward the cover of trees just ahead. The trail took them around a grouping of rocks and allowed them momentary cover from Mosely and the others.

Rain came from the dark clouds and splattered against the rocks as Dan rode higher, his horse wheezing from all the weight on its back. Dan knew Mosely and his men were mounting up and would be after them in a matter of moments. There was no way they could reach the cover of the trees on the hill before Mosely cut them off.

Dan reined up and pulled his rifle from its scabbard. He jumped down and told Clint to get into the saddle and lead Leslie and Ben Steiner to cover.

"What do you think you're doing?" Leslie asked.

"I'm going to slow them down," Dan said. "We

131

can't make the trees and I don't care to end it this way. Just ride ahead and I'll cover you."

"They'll kill you, Dan," Leslie said. "I'm staying here to help you."

"Go ahead like I asked you!" Dan said forcefully. "If we all stay here, we haven't got a chance. At least separated, we can come at them from two directions. Now, go!"

Leslie reluctantly rode with Clint and Ben Steiner toward the timber. Dan rushed to a better position overlooking the trail that would bring Mosely and the others pell-mell toward the hill just ahead. Thunder clapped overhead again and rain poured down.

Dan was ready when Mosely showed, though the rain made it hard to see them clearly. Mosely held them up and Dan refrained from firing until they were closer and easier to hit. He knew he had to shoot fast and make every shot count.

He was grateful that Mosely had stopped, for it gave Leslie and the two deputies that much more time to take a stand in the trees. But what was disturbing was the fact that Mosely was having his men spread out, thus giving them a better method of attack against the hill.

Dan got his rifle ready and squinted through the rain. He was going to have to shoot as well as he ever had in his life now. If he didn't, Mosely and his men would be by him and Leslie and the two deputies wouldn't stand a chance.

THIRTEEN

As the rain continued, Dan took careful aim and waited. As soon as the rider nearest him started forward, he would shoot. He wanted to wait until Mosely gave the word to charge. That way, when he opened up it would confuse them that much more.

Dan knew that Mosely wanted to get this over with as soon as possible. At the present time, Dan knew they stood a good chance of killing him, as well as Leslie and the two deputies. But darkness would fall before much longer and the odds of their winning this fight would be cut considerably.

Mosely sounded the charge and Dan's rifle spit fire through the rain. The rider nearest him fell backward off the horse, causing the others to rein in their own horses momentarily. This allowed Dan one more quick shot, dropping another of the horse hunters.

The rain came and the horse hunters stared at the bodies and tried to handle their fidgety horses. Mosely, a way over, was yelling at the men to continue on toward the trees. If they hesitated any longer, they would all be picked off one by one.

As they charged forward again, Dan dropped another rider and was preparing to shoot again. But the rain and the distance impaired his aim and he didn't fire. Instead, he ran along on foot, hoping to get up the hill and do some good from the rear.

As he ran along the slippery trail, he could hear gunfire coming through the storm from the trees. It was muffled, but Dan knew without question there was a major fight going on. Mosely and his men were yelling, trying to regroup. Then, from out of the rain, Dan saw three riders bearing down on him.

He was in the open and vulnerable. He scrambled for what little cover he could get behind a scrub juniper growing from a pile of rocks. He knew the riders had been sent back by Mosely to finish him, while the others hoped to get to Leslie and the deputies.

But the riders held up their horses—aware of Dan's deadly accuracy with his rifle—and dismounted. They crouched and watched him and pointed in different directions. Dan knew they did not intend to come straight on at him, but were spreading out instead, surrounding him from three sides.

Dan could not afford to move anywhere now. The rain was letting up some, not to his benefit, and there was nowhere for him to run. The three horse hunters had him blocked off from the hill, and he didn't want to go back down the trail; he would only be backing into a deeper trap.

The only way out of this, Dan realized, was to figure odds and angles accurately. If he could get two of the three men, he might be able to get to the hill, where Leslie and the two deputies were now making their own stand.

Dan watched the three as they split up, each taking a course of attack against him. One was coming straight on, moving cautiously from rock to rock as he made his way toward Dan's position. Dan decided this one was not the threat posed by the second man, who was hurrying to a position at an angle from where Dan was trapped behind the juniper.

The third man was moving quickly as well, but he had to, as he had more ground to cover to get into position to do any good with the other two. He moved with as much caution as he could, but exposed himself often in his hurry. All three of them were having trouble with the slippery footing.

The rain was lessening even more and the clouds lifted from a crimson horizon, where the setting sun had turned to fire. Dan realized the third man was going to have to hurry to get into position before the other two were ready to mount their attack and start shooting. If he allowed that, his chances of getting away alive would be slim.

Though every shot counted, Dan pulled and fired at the third man as he started to another rock. The bullet whined off the ground near him and Dan heard his startled yell. He stayed behind the rock for a good long time, which was what Dan hoped he would do.

The second man became restless and eager, showing himself to shoot. Dan crouched behind the juniper as the bullets clipped branches and whined off rocks, dangerously close. As the second man lowered himself to reload, Dan waited.

The third man was moving again, working his way more slowly and cautiously than before. He wouldn't pose a threat until he had reached his position.

But it was the first man that Dan now became concerned with.

Dan couldn't see him, though he knew the horse hunter was sitting somewhere close behind the juniper waiting for him to expose himself. Dan peered through the juniper foliage and saw the very tip of his rifle barrel sticking out from behind a rock.

Now was the time to act, Dan realized, if he was going to get the second man and not be shot by this one.

Dan aimed carefully at the exposed tip of the rifle, realizing the second gunman was nearly through reloading and was going to rise up and open fire at him again any second. Dan's rifle blast sounded and the bullet whined off the rifle, singing a whining metallic sound. The first gunman dropped the rifle.

Immediately, Dan swung around and aimed his rifle toward the position of the second man. As he had predicted, the gunman rose to open fire again. But Dan was ready and the bullet clipped the gunman square in the throat, entering just under his chin. His head tilted sideways as the bullet destroyed the back of his head and neck, and he fell in a heap to the ground.

Dan knew he had the element of fear and surprise on his side, and he rose and charged the position where the third gunman was still crouched. His only hope was that the first man hadn't recovered from having the rifle shot out of his hand yet.

As Dan ran he moved at angles, dodging back and forth. If the first gunman had recovered, he wouldn't have an easy target. And if the first gunman decided to fight and not run, he would be in the line of fire.

Dan was nearly to the third gunman's position when a rifle went off behind him. The first gunman had recovered. But Dan was dodging well enough that the shot missed.

The third gunman had just risen to shoot at Dan and the bullet from the first man's rifle whined off a rock near him. The third gunman froze.

Dan stopped and fired from the hip, blasting the horse hunter backward and into a spin. Dan levered in another round and turned, all in one motion. The first gunman was now at Dan's old position back near the juniper. He was getting ready to fire again when Dan's rifle cracked.

The bullet just missed him. It threw his aim off and he fired wildly, allowing Dan to take a new position where the third gunman lay near death. Dan levered in another round and found himself facing the juniper, thinking he now had the tables turned.

The gunfire from the hill behind him had

slowed considerably. He could hear the sounds of horses running and rose to see the stallion running his herd along the trail between the gunmen and him.

Dan knew that either way, he had to consider that bad. If Mosely and the others had succeeded in overrunning the hill, then Leslie and the deputies were likely dead. If not, then Mosely would be back down soon in retreat to pick up the other three. Then he wouldn't stand a chance.

Dan knew he had to act quickly. If he raised himself to fire at the third gunman behind the juniper, he could suffer the same fate as the dead man behind him. Dan reasoned that the gunman was just waiting—as he, himself, had waited—to see him rise to shoot.

Instead, Dan moved across the hard ground toward another section of rocks nearby. He drew fire from the one remaining gunman, but none of the bullets touched him. Then the gunman moved from behind the juniper and took another position, one where Dan couldn't see him.

Now it was a game of cat and mouse.

Dan knew the gunman was counting on Mosely and the others having stormed the hill successfully. He could now see the gunman working his way upslope through the rocks.

There was no more shooting going on, and there was no way to tell what had happened. But if Mosely had won the battle, then they would be coming back down very soon. Dan decided he had to cut the odds one way or another and gave chase to the one remaining gunman.

The gunman moved more quickly as Dan broke into a run, caring little about exposing himself entirely as he made his way up the hill. Dan knew the gunman would have to stop and expose himself as well if he was going to get a shot off.

And the gunman did just that, hoping to get a lucky shot off down the hill.

But Dan was waiting, and swung his .30-.30 to his shoulder as the gunman turned around to get his balance on the slick hillside. Dan's rifle cracked and the gunman yelled and clutched at his chest, his own rifle clattering from his bloody fingers into the rocks.

After reloading, Dan climbed the hill cautiously. The gunman lay still. He had toppled forward after being hit, and had rolled for a short distance, until stopped by a large rock. Now he lay at a twisted angle, his eyes staring up into the darkening evening sky.

The storm had passed and, as darkness approached, the late evening air grew still. He could hear men yelling just ahead of him and he recognized one of the voices as that of Claude Mosely. They were coming down.

They were upon him faster than he had anticipated and he fired quickly. He hit a rider right next to Mosely, and the man fell under Mosely's horse, causing everyone behind to veer off to avoid a pileup. Dan turned to run, but Mosely recovered his horse and led the others after him.

Dan could hear them bearing down, coming ever closer. He had just a way to go to get to the trees, but Mosely and the others were closing the distance.

Suddenly there was another sound, from just behind him and off to one side—the heavy sound of hooves against the hard-packed trail that came up out of the canyon. Dan turned to see the stallion and his herd thunder out of the canyon and up onto the open ridge.

The stallion saw Mosely and the others and bolted straight between Dan and the horse hunters. The herd followed, forming a solid line of running, squealing mustangs that roared across the open ridge and along the hill.

Dan took the opportunity to get out of the open and run up into the trees along the hillside. He could see Mosely and his men mixing in with the herd, racing their own horses to try to keep up. Dan saw no way he could stop them now.

When the herd had passed with Mosely and the horse hunters, Dan worked his way through the trees toward the top of the hill. There, he sneaked into the shadows. He feared the worst, for there was no sound. Then he heard the click of a hammer being pulled back on a rifle.

The blast sounded just as he dropped to his stomach. A pine branch snapped just above and behind him. Then he heard someone yelling.

"Don't come sneaking in here on us! We'll get you, we will!"

It was Leslie's voice. Dan yelled to her and she came to him immediately.

"What's happened up here?" Dan asked. "I

thought I would find you all dead."

"Mosely and the others left us to go down after you," Leslie explained. "The stallion came through here just as the storm was letting up, and I guess the horse hunters decided it was important to get him while they had the chance."

"It's a good thing the herd showed up when it did," Dan said. "I was caught out in the open. Where are Clint and Ben?"

"They're back where we made our stand. Clint's shoulder is bothering him, but none of us got hurt in the shootout we just had, thank God."

Dan walked with Leslie past the bodies of two horse hunters. Leslie said that they had gotten possibly three or four of them; she wasn't certain. But it had been dark enough in the trees to hold them off and stay well under cover.

"I was afraid you were dead," Leslie said.

"It was a close call," Dan admitted. "But now we've got other problems to think of, and we've got to figure out how to handle them."

"What about my sister and my folks?" Leslie asked. "Where do you think they are?"

"How well do they know this country?" Dan asked her.

"As well as anybody could."

"Then I'd say they're safe," Dan assured her. "At least for tonight. We'll have to find them tomorrow, though, so that Steadman doesn't get to them first."

"And the mustangs," Leslie said. "It looks like they ran right into Mosely and his men. They'll have them into that box canyon by tomorrow and there's no way we can stop them now. All Steadman will have to do is ride up here and it will be too late."

"Maybe," Dan said. "But we've got to worry about your folks before we do the stallion. They won't kill the stallion. And it will be hard for them to get the mustangs out of here as easily as they would have before."

Dan talked with Clint and Ben and got their stories, while Leslie prepared to make camp. Darkness had fallen, and the mountains now held only the sounds of crickets and night birds calling through the canyons.

They ate without benefit of a fire, in case some of the horse hunters came back to check up on them. But Dan wasn't so worried about Mosely and the others now. They had sustained heavy losses and their only concern would be to get the stallion into the box canyon and wait for Steadman to come up and get things over with.

Dan talked about it with Leslie as they went for a short walk across the high ridge. The moon—half full and bright—hung over the canyon. Leslie stayed close to him and looked into the sky. Finally, she took a deep breath and turned to Dan.

"This is only the beginning, isn't it?"

"I imagine things will get pretty tense from here on, yes," he answered.

"I don't know where any of my family is," she said, her voice filled with worry.

"We'll find them," Dan said. "My guess is

they're not far behind us, that they're likely on the way up to the box canyon. That's where everybody will be sooner or later."

"Do you really think so? But what if Steadman has them and wants to use them as hostages, like he did before?"

"We'll have to deal with everything as it happens," Dan said. "I won't put their lives in any danger, that I can promise you."

Leslie took another deep breath. She was sitting next to Dan on a large rock that overlooked the deep canyon country and took in the sweeping range of the mountains just behind them. On almost any other night, under almost any other circumstances, she would have been smiling.

"Would you promise me something else, Dan?" Leslie said to him.

"What's that?"

"Would you promise to bring me back up here again after this is all over? Then we can sit here again and look at the moon and the mountains, and we won't have to worry about anything. Will you promise me that?"

Dan looked into her eyes, filled with worry but also with a longing that she had been holding deep within her for a long time. She leaned toward him and he kissed her gently. Then he held her for a while.

"You don't belong up here," he finally told her. "Not like this. You've got to make a life for yourself. At least see some of the world and do some things. If you want to come back up here and live, then do it. But don't stay up here and miss out on your life."

Leslie looked at him again and her expression was calm. "This *is* my life, Dan. This is what I want. I know what the world has to offer and it's not for me. I've been down from these mountains some and there's no place I would ever want to stay longer than a few hours. I belong up here, and this is where I'll stay—helping my folks with their ranch."

Dan nodded. There was a certainty in her voice that told him she knew what she wanted and was sure of it. He could also tell that she was looking for someone to be with her, someone who knew the mountains and loved them as much as she did. And she knew finding someone like that was going to be difficult.

Leslie was looking out over the moonlit canyon once again. She watched a nighthawk sail by and become lost in the black sky. She seemed to know that Dan Slayter was the kind of man she wanted, but that he was committed to a life that would not suit her. She seemed to know he was certainly the kind of man she wanted, but could never have.

"Would you ever stop being a lawman and live in one place?" she finally asked.

"Maybe in time," Dan said. "I just don't know."

Leslie got up and turned to go back into camp. She stood nervously in front of Dan and finally pulled him to her and kissed him.

"If you ever want to quit sheriffing," she said, "think about coming back to these mountains, would you?" Then she turned and was lost in the shadows.

Before he went back to camp, Dan took one last look down into the canyon. He knew that tomorrow would bring a test that would tell whether or not he could rid these mountains of Nolan Steadman. And if he couldn't, that would mean he wouldn't get down out of here alive.

FOURTEEN

Steadman slept fitfully. The bed that belonged to Gus and Sadie Wilkens would not have been comfortable to him under any conditions. They had reached the ranch just before dark, only to find that no one was there. That meant either Sally and her parents were still somewhere in the mountains, or working their way down until everything was over.

Steadman also wondered if things were almost over, or if things were worse for them now than before. Upon reaching the ranch at dusk, they had heard shooting from far above them. There seemed little doubt that Claude Mosely had run into Slayter. What Steadman wanted to know in the worst way was whether Mosely had gotten Slayter.

But that problem couldn't be solved at least until the following morning. Traveling at night in the canyons was asking for a fall to your death. Intead of chancing going any farther, Steadman had opted to allow Keith Larson and the others to ransack the ranch house and then get some sleep.

It also bothered Steadman that Sally had gotten

away from Larson and the others. He was certain now that it had been old Gus and Sadie who had managed to free her. He should have given the old couple more credit.

But it bothered him more just to have her gone and hating him. She had adored him at one time, while he had simply used her. Now that she was gone, he wondered if he hadn't come to care for her more than he had thought. Though he didn't want to admit it to himself, he was feeling it.

It was something he thought about now as he tried to get some rest. He had killed men and disposed of them without any feeling for them whatsoever. He had known other women before Sally, and there had been nothing there, either. But with Sally, he had somehow learned something that reached into him, no matter how hard he tried to push it aside.

Sally had always been warm and trusting toward him. Even until the last few days, when she had become afraid for her folks, she had trusted him. Then he had broken that trust. Now she was gone, and he knew he wouldn't get her back.

As he thought more about it, his anger rose. If she didn't want him anymore, the he would see to it she didn't want anyone else, either. She couldn't just up and leave him like that and get away with it.

While he thought about it, he heard someone walking around in the kitchen. He left Gus and Sadie's bedroom and cocked his pistol as he sneaked out of the bedroom. He found Keith Larson sitting at the kitchen table, drinking from

148

a bottle in the dark.

"How do you expect to get any rest that way?" Steadman asked him. He struck light to a lantern.

"Can't rest as it is," Larson said. "We're in this thing deep." He handed the bottle to Steadman.

"We'll get out of it," Steadman assured him, gulping from the bottle and handing it back. "We'll get rid of Slayter and his lawmen. Then we'll meet up with Mosely and the others. They've likely got that stallion in the box canyon by now."

"I can't see how you figure it to be that easy," Larson said. "There's more than just Slayter and those other lawmen to worry about. Like as not they'll send up more lawmen."

"By then we'll have the stallion and we'll get him down out of here," Steadman said.

Larson had the bottle again and was drinking from it, looking at Steadman's face as the lantern light danced against his features. Larson noted how Steadman was saying one thing with his mouth, but his expression was saying another.

"You're as worried about it as I am," Larson told Steadman. "Why don't you admit it?"

"I said we'll get out of it!"

Steadman yelled and pounded his fist against the table, waking the rest of the men. A few of them burst into the kitchen from the living room with guns in their hands.

"Go back to sleep," Steadman told them. "We're just talkin', is all."

The men began to grumble, but settled back into sleep. Larson watched Steadman while he finished the bottle by himself, without offering him another drink. Larson finally brought up another concern of his.

"What about Sally?" he asked. "You figure we can catch up to her?"

"I don't care about that," Steadman said. "We've got to get up into the high country and meet Mosely and the others. Then we've got to get that stallion down out of there."

"I figure that Sally and her folks ain't that far ahead of us," Larson said. "What if we catch up to them?"

Steadman knew that Larson was wondering if he could actually kill the old couple if the need arose, and possibly Sally as well. There was no way Sally would ever let herself be caught by them again—not while she was still alive.

Steadman knew as well that Larson was still disgruntled about the first time he had held the old couple as hostages and had thought he could get Dan Slayter alone. Since that time, Steadman had decided he wouldn't try it by himself again, and he wanted Larson to be assured of that.

"We'll catch up to old Gus and Sadie," Steadman said. "And if Sally's still with them, we'll get her, too. This time you'll help me get Slayter." Steadman was looking at Larson while he spoke. "Is that what you wanted to hear?"

"Just so we get Slayter," Larson said flatly. "I don't care what else happens, just so we get Slayter."

Dan led the way, his eyes watching everything

that moved in the hills and anyone around them. They rode across the upper Bighorn Mountains, just below high peaks that rose into the clouds, the highest still capped with snow. Eagles soared in high circles overhead, screaming out across the timbered canyons below.

Dan knew that Leslie and the young deputies were getting ever more tense as they followed the tracks where the horse hunters had taken the herd after the shootout the evening before. It had been a close call that easily could have cost all of them their lives. And it was certain that Claude Mosely and the horse hunters with him would be on close lookout from now on.

Leslie often asked to stop and look over the country behind them and on all sides, where there was any possibility that her sister and folks might be. She knew they would not stay down at the ranch. It would be far too dangerous to stay anywhere near Steadman and the other men who had killed Chris Benson and the deputies. Steadman was loose again and he would be a lot more determined about killing whoever got in his way.

As they traveled across the tops of the canyons, Dan knew the problem of Steadman coming up from below and Claude Mosely being just above them was serious. Steadman would be coming fast and Mosely would no doubt be waiting. He would be in the middle with Leslie and two inexperienced deputies, one of whom was wounded.

Though Clint didn't complain, Dan could see that the wound in the top of his shoulder was bothering him tremendously. And there was no way to get him down below without waiting for the SWAT team to arrive in the helicopter.

They had been trying continuously to reach the Lovell office on their radios, but the interference was making it impossible to get their calls through. The canyons and the timber, together with the distance, were too much to allow the calls to reach the dispatcher.

Dan couldn't help but think that Williams and the backup help would make it before long. Though it was almost impossible to assemble a team when there were a lot of other problems going, Williams had promised to make the Steadman case the main priority.

And it was time they arrived. Dan knew they were closing in on the horse hunters and the herd of wild mustangs. There were fresh tracks everywhere. It would be only a short time until they found them. Then the trick would be to get the stallion and the herd and drive them down below and back toward the wild horse range.

Claude Mosely and the bunch with him would no doubt be a problem. But after losing as many men as they had, Dan was certain they would fight a more conservative battle this time. Dan knew Mosely couldn't lose any more men and still be able to catch the stallion.

Dan stopped often to glass the many pockets of timber and rock for any sign of horses or horse hunters. There was a lot of country to cover and Dan worried that they would not get over it all until it was too late.

They rode on and turned their horses down into

a large canyon where the trail was worn deep. The trail had been used often and was embedded with fresh tracks. Where it led was anybody's guess.

Leslie pointed far down to where the canyon came out onto the wild horse range. There was a lot of country between, and the stallion and the herd were bound to be somewhere amid the maze of small pockets of grass and water that were interspersed with little canyons and isolated rock formations.

Dan led them down the trail cautiously. There were a lot of places where riflemen could place themselves and make it hard to come out of the place alive.

They went just a short way farther and came into a series of small canyons that merged with the main canyon, where a stream of water traced its way down through rocks and small flats covered with grass and scrub timber. The main trail went through the bottom with branches going up the various smaller side canyons.

The fresh tracks broke off the main trail and led up one of the small canyons. Dan took them up into it and they found themselves in a narrow gorge where rock walls rose vertically along both sides of the trail, until they encircled a large, grassy flat.

It was a box canyon, where springs gushed from the rocks and grass sprang green and moist. Across the entrance a pole fence was fashioned that connected to the rock walls on both sides and edged down the slope to a large gate across the trail. The gate was now closed tightly.

The canyon went a good distance back, and into a narrow passageway that broke out again into a small meadow. Far back in the reaches of the canyon were the mustangs, held captive behind the fence of poles. The question now was whether or not Claude Mosely and the remaining horse hunters with him were back in the canyon with the horses.

Dan saw little sense in going back into the canyon to find out. If the horse hunters were there, they would certainly be waiting. An ambush in this canyon, Dan thought, was not something they could escape from so easily as out in the open.

He saw little else they could do but open the pole gate and swing it back. If the horse hunters were not in there, the stallion might find his way out. Otherwise, the herd would remain there until Steadman and the others rejoined Claude Mosely and those with him.

Dan saw little that they could do now but wait. And he worried even about that, as there were still a lot more men than they could stand off.

To complicate things more, Steadman could show up at any time and make the odds that much worse.

Dan saw a trail that led up and around the edge of the box canyon. He decided the best thing they could do was to take the trail and move cautiously around to where they could see down into the bottom. The more they knew about the canyon and what was in it, the better.

They rode the trail, staying away from the edge where it overlooked the bottom. Dan didn't think they could afford to project themselves against the skyline and allow whoever was down there to see them. It would be better if they saw whoever was down there first.

Dan stopped them at a place where they could peer over the edge and not be seen. They took position, and Dan glassed down into the canyon. There he could see the stallion pacing in circles, while the herd fed on what grass was left by a small stream.

Near the stream was an old cabin. Tied outside were horses belonging to Claude Mosely and the remainder of the horse hunters. It was an old line shack now being used by Steadman and his men as a way station from which they caught horses and moved them out for sale.

"Let's go back down and take those horses out of there," Leslie suggested. She was angry and her words came out hard.

"We should know more about this canyon first," Dan said. "There's no way we could go down in there and hope to come out alive if we don't know as much as they do about this country around here. And there're a lot more of Mosely's men than there are of us."

"If we wait too long, they'll take the stallion," Leslie warned.

"We haven't got a choice," Dan said. "We can't do this alone. We have to have help."

They rode farther up the trail and, when they realized they were looking down into the end of the canyon, they dismounted again.

"That's why they're successful in catching so

155

many horses," Leslie pointed out, looking at the steep layers of vertical rock.

They were at the very top of a steep incline. All around them, resting at the edge of the cliff, were large boulders. Right below them was a high, rocky hill that ascended from the bottom. It was the only way out of the back end of the canyon. Horses and other livestock could never make it. Anyone who wanted out on foot could make it, but with great difficulty. It was indeed a good trap for catching wild horses.

They studied the canyon below them for a time, aware that the horse hunters were a way down and that they didn't use this end until they caught the horses. Dan was pointing to different locations where deputies could take cover, when Leslie nudged him and pointed to dust coming up from below.

It was still a distance away, but it was the dust of many riders. The riders were no doubt Steadman and his men, coming up through a different canyon.

They mounted and rode into the cover of nearby timber that overlooked the other canyon. Suddenly, Leslie was again pointing to an open area below a long slope that rose to meet the summit. She was shielding her eyes from the sun and showing Dan where she could see riders ahead of the dust.

Dan put his field glasses to his eyes and looked long and hard. He could recognize the lead rider easily—Nolan Steadman.

"They're riding awful hard," Dan commented.

Clint Phillips turned everyone's attention to three other riders not far ahead of Steadman and his men. Three riders whom everyone immediately recognized.

"It's Sally and my folks," Leslie said, her voice mixed between the exhilaration of knowing where they were and the fear of watching them being caught by Steadman and the others.

Dan lowered his glasses and watched the dust in the distance draw ever closer. "We can help them," he said. "But we've got to be watching both sides. If Claude Mosely hears something, he and his men will come up and out of that canyon, and they'll be ready to shoot."

"Don't think I'm not ready to shoot," Leslie said quickly. "Nothing's going to stop me from helping them get away from Steadman."

FIFTEEN

Dan was watching Steadman's men coming up the steep trail when Clint Phillips suddenly gave Dan his radio. The reception was poor and it broke up often, but Dan could understand that the SWAT team was on its way. He picked up that there would be two helicopters, one with the SWAT team and another to follow that would fly in Williams and some FBI men.

The news sparked enthusiasm in the entire group. They knew if they could get Sally and Gus and Sadie safely up the trail with them, and hold off Steadman and his men, the rest of the problems should work themselves out.

But now the hard part was to keep Steadman from getting to Sally and Gus and Sadie.

Dan prepared to lead Leslie and the deputies to a group of rocks overlooking the trail where Sally and the old couple were working their horses up the trail, trying to stay ahead of Steadman.

"We can take position over there." Dan was pointing, showing how they could look down on anyone coming up the trail.

"Do you think we can hold Steadman and the rest of them off until Sally and our folks get up the trail?" Leslie asked.

"We can't go down in there and hope to accomplish anything," Dan pointed out. "We'll just have to do the best we can from where we are."

"What about Claude Mosely and the other bunch of horse hunters in the box canyon?" Leslie asked Dan. "What if they do come out after us?"

"We can't worry about them now," Dan told her. "We've got to get Sally and your folks with us, and then be ready for Mosely and the others. Hopefully, the SWAT team will be here by then."

Dan led the way, opening his horse up to a dead run across an open meadow to where the switch-back through the canyon met the summit. Leslie was right behind him, holding her rifle in her free hand. She would fight to the end for her family, no matter what might happen.

Dan watched while Sally led her folks through the last switchback in the trail. She had been looking back to where Steadman and his men were coming up as fast as they could. But she turned when Leslie called down to her, and waved her free hand with a yell of surprise.

Once on top, Sally, Gus and Sadie all kicked their horses into a run. Leslie rode to meet them and they all jumped down from their horses and into one another's arms.

"Thank God," Leslie said. "Up until a short time ago, I was afraid Steadman would catch you."

"They just about caught us in camp this morning," Sally explained. "We're lucky they didn't see us until we'd gotten a good headstart. But now I don't know how we're going to stand them all off."

Gus held up his Sharps rifle. "I've got an idea how we can keep them off us," he said. "This here old buffalo gun shoots a mile."

Leslie took them over to where Dan and the deputies had taken position in the rocks overlooking the switchback trail below. Steadman and the others were making their way up. They were still out of rifle range—ordinary rifle range—and Gus settled in beside Dan with his old .50 Sharps.

"This ought to make them sit up and take notice," Gus said with a smile.

"We can't just open up on them," Dan told him. "I'll give them a chance to surrender."

"You ain't going to think for a minute they'd surrender?" Gus asked, his mouth gaping.

"I have to give them that option," Dan said.

Steadman and his men were coming around the last curve of the switchback, getting ready to kick their horses into a faster gait as they came up on top. Dan shouted down into the canyon and told Steadman to stop and put his hands up into the air.

But Steadman was not about about to give himself up, and turned his horse, yelling at the others to take cover.

Dan yelled again and when some of the horse hunters started shooting, Dan nodded to Gus, who smiled and took aim with his Sharps. The big gun boomed and one of Steadman's men was literally blown out of the saddle. Dan dropped one of them

161

with his own rifle.

Leslie and the deputies began to fire as well. One of the bullets tore through Steadman's upper arm. He cursed and got behind cover with his men, so well behind cover that they could not see the top, nor could anyone on top see them.

Despite the fact there were none of Steadman's men showing themselves, Gus decided he would give them a demonstration of the gun's power anyway. He loaded and fired the single-shot weapon a number of times, blowing the trunks away from small trees near where Steadman and his men were hiding, and blasting large rocks into fragments. It was apparent to anyone watching why a bullet from the old Sharps had once knocked down buffalo at a long distance with a single shot.

Steadman moved his men farther down the canyon, leading their horses and staying under cover. Gus almost got one of the horse hunters, blowing a large gouge in the face of a rock just over the man's head.

When Steadman and his men had retreated to where there was little chance they would do any harm, Dan thought about their next move. He thought about going down into the canyon and trying to get Steadman again. But he realized it would be endangering his life as well as the lives of the two deputies and the Wilkens family. They had been too close to death as it was and he didn't want to get them involved in stopping Steadman and the others.

In fact, he wanted to get them away from

Steadman as quickly as possible.

Suddenly, Clint Phillips shouted and pointed to where Mosely and the other group of horse hunters were coming out of the box canyon.

"They heard us shooting," Leslie said. "Now what do we do?"

"I'll just send them back down where they came from," old Gus said, setting the sights on the Sharps. "I'll send them back to hell."

Gus fired the big gun, aiming for Mosely. The bullet went just over his left shoulder and took most of the head off one of the riders just behind him. Mosely and his men scattered like a flock of grouse.

Gus fired again, dropping a horse hunter from the saddle at nearly four hundred yards. Finally, Mosely's men were far out across the top of the ridge, taking cover in the trees.

"That will slow them down," Dan said. "But sooner or later they'll regroup and figure a way to come at us from different sides."

"They'll by God have to swing out a good mile before they get out of my range," Gus said.

Dan gave it careful thought and decided his chief consideration should be the safety of the Wilkenses and getting Clint Phillips to a doctor. The wound in the top of his shoulder would become infected soon if he didn't get medical attention.

"I want all of you to head back down through that other canyon," Dan told them. "Mosely and the others are a way out yet and Steadman and his bunch are still down below in this canyon. That will give you a lot of time to get a good headstart down out of here. Take the opportunity and go."

"I want to be in on this until the end," Gus said.

"It's not worth risking your life over," Dan told him. "Go, now while you have the chance."

Clint Phillips spoke up and handed Dan his radio. "If the SWAT team and the others haven't arrived by the time we get down below, I'm coming back up." Ben Steiner nodded and said he would join him.

"You two just get everybody down out of here and we'll talk about it all when it's over," Dan said.

"What about you?" Leslie asked. "That will leave you all alone."

"The SWAT team will be here at any time now," Dan said. "I just want all of you away from Steadman and all his men. Now, hurry and get going."

Gus handed Dan the Sharps and a box of shells. "You won't be alone."

"I can't take that," Dan said.

"Take it anyway," Gus insisted. "You'll need it; we won't."

"What makes you so sure?" Dan asked. "Steadman and the men with him are just a canyon over from you."

"That's true," Gus said with a nod, "but everybody knows there's only two things here Steadman is really interested in: you and that black stallion. He wants both of you real bad and he don't care about anything else right now. So, take the gun and use it."

Dan took the rifle and rode over to the edge of the other canyon, where Gus led the others down a hidden trail that would take them toward the bottom. Leslie looked back and her face held concern. Dan waved them all on and turned his horse back up toward the top.

His concern now was to get the stallion out of the box canyon and on the way down Devil Canyon toward the wild horse range. He hoped that he could get it done and that the SWAT team would arrive to help him round up Steadman and his men.

But time was not on his side, as it would be difficult to get down into the box canyon and free the horses before Steadman went with Mosely and the others. Dan was determined, though, and he kicked his horse into a dead run. They could all rest when this was over.

Steadman was cursing, looking at the bullethole through his arm. It was a flesh wound, but it had bled a lot The muscles were now cramping some and he knew he would have to work the arm continuously to keep it from being useless to him. He couldn't afford that now, not with Dan Slayter standing between him and the stallion.

"Damn the luck!" Steadman said, trying to wrap a bandage around his arm.

"Just be glad that old bastard, Gus, never hit you with that Sharps," Larson said. "He blew Vince in half."

Steadman reflected on the horse hunter who had

been shot out of the saddle back up the canyon. Steadman finished with the bandage and looked up the trail. There was no way to know where Slatyer and the old man and the rest of them were, and it would be foolish to ride up and find out. The Sharps was a deadly weapon—even if it was well over a hundred years old.

"Do you figure they'll keep us pinned down here?" Larson asked.

"Hell, I don't know what they're up to," Steadman said, holding his arm. "All I know is I plan to see every last one of them dead."

"You should have killed that old man when you had the chance," Larson pointed out.

Steadman turned on him and his lips were curled back. "I don't want to hear no more about that—understand? I know I should have done things different, but that's past. Now we have to figure how we're goin' to get ourselves out of this mess."

One of the other men spoke up. "Where do you figure Mosely and the others are? We ain't that far from the box canyon."

Steadman thought about it. Mosely and the others certainly should have trapped the stallion by now. They were most likely in the canyon waiting for them. But if they had heard the shooting, they would certainly come up to see what was going on.

"Maybe we'd ought to go down a ways and pick up that trail a ways back down that goes out to the top," Larson suggested. "That way we could come around and stay in the trees mostly. We can't let that old man shoot any more with his Sharps."

Steadman thought just a short time before he agreed that to try to go up the same trail could be asking for more Sharps rifle bullets. The old man was a deadly aim and there was no room for error on the steep trail through the canyon.

However, going back and up onto the top would keep them under cover and allow them to come around on Slayter and the others. And if Mosely and the others had come out of the box canyon to see what the shooting was all about, they could get Slayter and the others trapped between them.

Steadman began to get eager. He took the men back down the trail to where it connected with another trail that wound up out of the canyon and onto the top. They were still a good way from where they had originally spotted Slayter and the others, but at least they would not be out in the open if Gus Wilkens saw them and opened up again with his Sharps.

As they rode, Steadman made sure they were under cover of trees or rocks all the time. His arm was bothering him, but he tried to ignore it and focus his attention on finding Slayter and the others. He knew Slayter well enough now to know that wouldn't be easy.

They got to the rocks above the canyon where Gus Wilkens had devastated them so badly with his Sharps. Steadman led them into position so that they could shoot into the rocks without presenting a target of themselves. But there was no sign of anybody there now.

"Where do you suppose they went?" Larson

asked Steadman.

Steadman was irritated. He rubbed his arm and looked the country over. "I don't know where the hell they went," Steadman finally said. "Where's Mosely and the others?"

Steadman hadn't much more than asked the question when one of the men with him pointed to riders coming from near a thick grove of trees. It was Mosely, and he was leading the men with him in a slow, deliberate search across the top. When they saw Steadman and the others, they came across at a fast gallop.

"Where've you been?" Mosely asked Steadman bluntly.

"We've been gettin' ourselves shot up," Steadman said. "And it wouldn't have happened if you'd been around to help us."

"We've got the stallion down in the canyon," Mosely explained. "We've been up here better'n two days wondering what's kept you. When we hear shooting and come out to check on it, Stan Mason gets his head blown off. And you say *you've* been shot up!"

"It's Gus Wilkens and his Sharps rifle," Steadman said. "We didn't expect him to get brave like that. He got a couple of the boys with me, too. But where's he at now—he and Slayter and the others?"

"We ain't seen them at all, not since they opened up on us," Mosely said. "We had to head way out for cover when the old man started shooting. But then he quit and it's been real quiet."

Steadman was looking all around again. "I

don't like this at all. They could be anywhere."

He told his men to spread out and cover the entire top well, and to travel very slowly and look well before they rode anywhere that could be an ambush.

"I don't know where they're at," Larson said. "But I don't want Slayter goin' down out of here alive."

SIXTEEN

Dan made his way down into the box canyon, looking for signs that any of the horse hunters had remained behind. It was possible, though not entirely likely. The stallion and his herd were securely fenced in the canyon and Mosely would feel there was no need to worry about them.

If his plan worked, Dan would soon be watching the stallion and his herd rushing out of the canyon and toward freedom once again.

He rested the Sharps rifle across the pommel of his saddle and studied the canyon. He stopped and used his field glasses frequently to survey the canyon walls and the tree cover in front of him. As he rode, he noted every possible location for a lookout or where men could position themselves to shoot down on the trail.

Dan finally decided that if Mosely had left men behind, either he would have spotted them or they would be shooting by now. He was nearing the gate to the enclosure that had been built across the bottom of the canyon. The small cabin was just ahead and there were no horses with saddles

171

anywhere near. Everyone had left to investigate the earlier gunshots and he had the whole canyon to himself now. Dan couldn't believe he was just going to ride up to the gate and open it without any resistance.

But it fit. Up until two days before, Steadman and his men had been so brash and reckless about their control over this high canyon country that they wouldn't have dreamed anyone would challenge them. Now they were going to see that the end for their whole operation was nearly at hand.

Dan got down from his horse, still watching for movement along the canyon walls above him. He opened the big pole gate and swung it back wide. He wanted to take the time to tear the entire fence out, but he was pushing his luck as it was.

Now there was no time to waste. He kicked his horse into a gallop and rode up toward the herd. The stallion shook his head and laid his ears back flat. The big black was annoyed at having been tricked into the box canyon and was ready to fight anyone who would try to catch him.

Dan sat his horse and admired the big stallion for a time. He knew he would never get this close to the horse again and he wanted to make the time last as long as possible. But he realized that time was fast running out.

Finally, Dan circled around the horses, driving them toward the gate. The stallion merely loped for a distance, but when he saw the open gate, he hit full stride immediately.

The mares followed him, straining to keep up. They made a long line that raised dust high in to the sky above the canyon floor. They kicked and squealed in their newfound freedom. To them, getting out from behind the gate and out of the canyon was the most important thing they could possibly do now.

Dan had no idea where Steadman and the others were at the present time. But he knew there was no doubt that they would see the dust and come immediately—he just hoped he could get out with the horses and get them started on the trail back down toward the horse range before the horse hunters all showed up.

The stallion ran down toward the entrance to the canyon. They would soon be out of the narrowest part and into a more open bottom. Dan followed them closely, then finally worked his own into the tail end of the herd. They were almost there, and it felt good to think the black stallion would soon be loose for good.

But as the herd approached the mouth of the canyon, Dan could see a lot of riders coming down, blocking the trail. Steadman and Mosely had been closer than Dan had expected, and they had joined forces. Now there was no place for the stallion to go.

The stallion squealed and turned in a tight circle as a dozen men with ropes whirling turned him back. In the confusion, the stallion ran into one of the mares, stumbled, and twisted its leg in the rocks off the side of the trail.

Dan saw the horse go down, then regain its balance and try to run ahead. But the big black was hurt, and Dan knew if the horse hunters pushed the stallion any harder, they could kill or permanently injure the horse.

Instead of trying to escape in the dust and confusion, Dan rode between the horse hunters and the injured stallion. Surprised at seeing him, they turned off and allowed the stallion and the confused herd to mill about and finally settle down in the close confines of the bottom.

Dan quickly found himself surrounded by Steadman and his men. They all held rifles on him and he expected to hear them shooting at any moment.

Instead, Steadman rode forward with his rifle pointed at Dan's middle. Dan could see where the bulletwound now had begun to swell and deform his arm. But Steadman didn't seem to notice, such was his glee at catching Dan.

"Looks like you just about made it out with our horses," he said with a twisted smile. "Where did you think you were goin' to take them?"

"Back down to the wild horse range, where they belong," Dan answered.

Steadman laughed. He pointed to the stallion, standing with its sides heaving and its lame leg raised slightly. "No, that horse belongs to me. You ought to know that by now."

"You don't care much about your horses," Dan told him. "Not if you treat them like that."

"He'll be fine," Steadman said with indifference. "It's not for you to worry about."

Keith Larson had been watching closely. He rode up to where Steadman was sitting his horse, gloating over his capture of Dan Slayter.

"Why don't we just shoot him and get it over with?" Larson asked.

Steadman turned to Larson. "Because I aim to give him some of the same medicine he gave me down below. That's why."

Larson looked up into the sun. "I'd think the heat was getting to you, or a rattler bit you," Larson said. "The only good sense is to shoot that lawman. There's others on their way, you know."

"What I want to do to him won't take long," Steadman insisted. "He's going to die in a bad way. Now, got get his guns and tie his hands behind him."

Larson did as he was instructed, eyeing Steadman as he took first the Sharps and then the .30-.30. He took the pistol and, with the help of another horse hunter, tied Dan's hands behind him with a length of rope.

After Larson had completed his task, he reined his horse in beside Steadman and talked to him in a low voice.

"You'd just as well untie him and give his guns to him if you don't aim to kill him right now," Larson warned. "We got him. Let's not waste it."

"How many times have I got to tell you that I give the orders around here?" Steadman growled.

Larson turned away and took a deep breath.

"How's he goin' to get away from us?" Steadman asked Larson. "We've got guns on him from all sides. And he's tied up so tight he can't spit. What's your worry?"

"All I'm sayin' is that he's apt to pull something," Larson answered. "Look what's happened

175

before—and he's not dead yet. Think about it."

Steadman looked from Larson to where Dan calmly sat his horse, his hands tied behind him. "Let me go over and see what Slayter thinks of all this," Steadman told Larson.

Dan had overheard most of what Steadman and Larson had been talking about. He knew Larson was fit to be tied, and that he was certain the best thing to do was shoot first and then be concerned about revenge.

Up to now, Steadman hadn't been listening. Steadman's ego was working overtime again. Dan knew that was the only thing that kept Steadman from killing him right away, as anyone with any sense would.

But Steadman was fast losing whatever sense he had once had. For this reason, Larson wasn't about to give up. He was going to insist that they kill him quickly. Dan just hoped Steadman had complete control of the gang.

He had seen the yearning to shoot embedded in Larson's face earlier as the men had surrounded him. And he had also noticed the disgust that covered Larson's face when Steadman had told them he wanted no one to open fire.

Steadman stopped his horse and Dan waited for him to speak.

"We're holding a meeting," Steadman said. "You're going to die today, but we're all deciding just when that will happen. Do you have any suggestions?"

Steadman laughed and turned his horse around. He rode back to where Larson sat waiting.

"I've thought about it," Steadman said. "I want him to die slow, and that's the way it will be. Then we'll throw him off into the canyon with the others."

"Suit yourself," Larson grumbled, and rode away with Dan's guns.

"Not so fast," Steadman said. "Come back here with that Sharps."

He took the rifle from Larson, while Larson frowned and turned away again.

"What about these?" Larson asked, holding up the .30-.30 and the pistol. "Do I get them?"

"We'll decide who gets those when we get that stallion down out of here," Steadman replied dryly. "If you wouldn't sass so much, you might get a favor or two. Now, take a few of the men and drive them horses back up where they belong."

"Have Mosely do it," Larson suggested. "He's the one got them in here."

"I want *you* to do it, Larson," Steadman insisted. "Take anybody you want, but *you* go along."

Larson frowned and took some men with him while he trailed the mustangs back up into the canyon and through the gate. It was hard to tell how badly the stallion was hurt. But it would be at least a few days until the horse could walk very well, and likely a lot more time before he could run.

When Larson was gone with the others, Steadman again rode over to where Dan sat on his horse, his hands tied tightly behind him.

"This will be a lot of fun," he said to Dan. "I'm

lookin' forward to it."

"What have you got planned?" Dan asked calmly.

"It ain't no picnic," Steadman answered. "Not for you it ain't. But when I'm done with you, the buzzards will have a lot to be happy about." He laughed. "Yeah, they'll have one hell of a picnic."

The ride down toward the bottom was slow and dangerous. As in the other canyons, there were rattlesnakes everywhere, and during the day they would be down near the water.

They had no choice but to ride the trail, which crossed the little stream a number of times. Often they would hear buzzing, and it got to the point where Leslie had to get down and beat the grass with a stick before traveling into it.

Though the snakes were a problem, Sally had other things on her mind. There was still no sign of a helicopter or reinforcements coming from anywhere. They had ridden less than halfway down when Sally suddenly stopped and turned her horse around.

"I've got to go back up there," she announced. "I've got to put an end to all of this. And I'm the only one that can do it."

Leslie stared at her sister. Everyone was shocked. They were now all out of danger and Sally was talking about riding back up into it all again.

"How do you intend to put an end to all of it?" Leslie asked.

"It's too hard to explain," Sally said. "I've just got to go back up."

Leslie looked to Gus and Sadie. Both of them were just as puzzled. But Sally was getting ready to turn back. She got down and filled her canteen in the creek.

"Don't anybody try to stop me," she said. "None of you know why I'm going back up there and none of you would understand. Just let me do what I want."

"Sally, you could be killed," her mother said. "We all have come close to getting killed already. What's the matter with you?"

"I told you, there isn't time to explain," Sally said. She was getting onto her horse once more.

"I can't let you go alone," Leslie finally said. "I'm going back up there with you, for whatever reason you've chosen."

"No, not both of you," Gus said.

"We'll make it back," Leslie told him. "Go on back to the ranch with Clint and Ben and wait for more lawmen to come. We'll be back down before long. I know we will."

Leslie rode with Sally toward the top once again. They rode in silence for a way and Leslie finally asked Sally what possessed her to go back up, and how she thought she could put an end to all of it.

Sally thought for a time before she finally answered. "I don't know how to tell you just yet," she finally replied. "I just know that I have to go back up there and try to talk Nolan into stopping

179

this foolishness."

"Don't tell me you still love him, not after all this!" Leslie said.

"I'm not sure," Sally told Leslie. "I'm just not sure at all. But I do know something's changed with me and I want to stop all of this. And I know I can."

SEVENTEEN

Dan felt the barrel of the Sharps rifle poking him in the spine as he rode across the top, with Steadman just behind him. Steadman was taking them to where they had thrown the other bodies deep into the upper end of Devil Canyon. It would be a suitable place to end things for Dan, also—at least that was what Steadman wanted.

He wanted to end it with Dan going far over into the depths where no one would find him. It would be suitable—the big lawman who got lost in the high Bighorns and was never found.

Steadman was overconfident. He was laughing and taunting Dan as they rode, asking him how it felt to know he was going to die within a short time.

"Ever have this happen to you before?" Steadman asked Dan. "Ever think you were goin' to see the big blue sky for the last time?"

"Never," Dan answered. "And I don't feel that way this time, either."

Steadman gouged him in the back with the barrel of the Sharps. "Well, you'd better feel that way. I'm going to beat you to nothing, then blow your head off with this buffalo gun. How does that sound?''

"You'd better do it now," Dan told him. "If you wait, who knows what could happen."

Steadman's face reddened and his grip tightened on the rifle. But he realized if he shot Dan then and there, he would be losing out on the satisfaction of having beaten Dan badly, the way he, himself, had been beaten. He wanted to deal out as much punishment as he could—not just end things with a quick pull of the trigger.

And he knew Dan Slayter was certain he wouldn't shoot him, or he would have by now. Slayter was only stalling for time, Steadman realized, hoping there would be someone to come along to save him.

Steadman noticed also that Keith Larson was still frowning. But Steadman didn't care if Larson's logic was sound. Maybe he should just shoot Dan Slayter and not take any chances. But that wasn't going to happen.

They rode the edge of the canyon, Dan feeling the tip of the Sharps rifle barrel continuously. He could sense Steadman's uneasiness, mixed with the anger he displayed continuously. Finally, Steadman stopped his horse and looked over the edge into the seemingly endless dropoff.

"Down there is a good place for your grave," he said with a laugh.

"Maybe you'll end up down there with me," Dan told him.

Steadman's face turned hard and he ordered

Larson to get Dan down off his horse.

"I want to give you worse—a lot worse—than you gave me the other day," Steadman said to Dan. "And I'm goin' to enjoy myself."

Larson pulled Dan off his horse and pushed him to the ground. But Dan was up quickly. Steadman's men got off their horses and gathered around. But Dan was facing them and there was no one holding him.

"Grab him," Steadman said to the horse hunters.

Three of them stepped forward. One bigger man was in the lead and the other two came on both sides of him. Dan waited until just the right instant to slam his right boot into the bigger man's knee, causing him to scream and slump to the ground.

The other two hesitated and then came on, helped by three others this time. They managed to overpower Dan and hold him upright. Then Steadman smiled and came forward.

Dan turned and twisted as best he could, but he was unable to defend himself against the savage pounding Steadman was now dishing out. Larson and one other horse hunter held Dan by the elbows as Steadman landed blow after blow in Dan's face and stomach.

Dan was soon a mass of welts and cuts along his face and head, and sore along his ribs and inside his stomach cavity from the blows that Steadman dealt him. His only salvation was the fact that Steadman took time between his attacks to stand back and tell Larson and the others that they were all witnessing the end of Dan Slayter, and the end of a lawman whose reputation was too big.

Dan would rise to his feet and catch his breath, fighting off the pain, while Steadman stood back and pointed.

"He ain't so much, is he?" Steadman would ask his men whenever he took time out from hitting Dan. "This lawman ain't so big as what folks would have you believe."

Steadman started in on him again and Dan quickly saw that if he kept rising to his feet, Steadman was going to beat him to death even before he threw him over the cliff. Steadman would hit him repeatedly and Dan would rise, defying Steadman's power.

Dan soon realized that coming to his feet repeatedly was only enraging Steadman. He might be buying time, but soon Steadman would take to using his boots on him.

To avoid it, Dan finally stayed on the ground. Steadman laughed with Larson and the others, and finally suggested they throw him over the edge and get it all over with.

Steadman stood back while some of the men again came forward. They were more cautious this time. Keith Larson broke in among them and told them he wanted to get his rope first.

Dan felt Larson working at the bonds holding his hands behind his back, twisting the knots until they loosened and finally came free. It took some time, and Steadman grumbled. But Larson pointed out that he didn't want to cut the rope—it was just right for tying people up and he had already lost one when Gus and Sadie Wilkens had freed Sally down the canyon a way.

Dan waited until Larson had unwrapped the last coil of rope and was dragging him toward the edge with the other horse hunters. Then, just before the edge, Dan made his move.

He rose, knocking both Larson and the other man aside. Larson toppled backward, catching himself just before going over the edge, but the other man kept his balance and came at Dan. With one quick movement, Dan moved aside and shoved the horse hunter into a tumble over the edge of the canyon.

Larson moved back from Dan while Steadman and the others stood staring. They couldn't believe Dan had taken that kind of beating and still had the strength to fight off two men.

Finally, Steadman started forward toward Dan and the other horse hunters encircled him. Dan was waiting, his fists raised.

"You're going to have to shoot me, Steadman," Dan said. "I won't go over any other way."

"You think you can hold all of us off?" Steadman asked.

"Do what he wants," Larson said. "Shoot him."

Steadman held up his hand. "I'm handling this."

He ordered his men to go toward Dan with him. Dan waited for the right moment, then began lashing out at the men with Steadman. He was at the edge of the canyon, where the footing was most treacherous. Two of them rushed him and Dan dealt one of them a powerful blow, sending him into a spin that caused him to lose his balance and also go over the edge.

But the other horse hunter grabbed Dan from behind and climbed up on his back. Steadman yelled and came forward. Dan saw his chance then to get Steadman.

With the horse hunter on his back, trying to claw at his eyes, Dan tackled Steadman. As he rammed Steadman, Dan lowered his head and the man on his back slammed his face into Steadman's chin. Dazed, the horse hunter on Dan's back released his grip and slid off.

Steadman was also reeling from the blow and Dan held onto him until they were just at the edge of the canyon. As he shoved Steadman, two other men pushed him from behind and he nearly fell over the edge, but caught himself on a sagebrush plant.

Steadman also caught himself as he went over, by grabbing the branches of a creeping juniper bush. He dangled over the edge, yelling, while some of his men came to save him. Larson went to Steadman's horse and got the Sharps rifle.

Steadman was on top again, regaining his breath from his near-miss with death.

"Shoot him!" Larson yelled at Steadman, holding out the rifle to him. "For Christ's sake, shoot him!"

Dan rose from his hands and knees, where he was regaining his strength once more. He saw Steadman take the rifle from Larson and reload. Steadman cocked the hammer back and raised th rifle.

"Somebody's comin', Nolan. Look, somebody's comin'!"

One of the horse hunters was pointing to where two riders were racing their horses toward them. Steadman recognized Sally and Leslie right away, and stared as they reined in their horses.

Sally jumped down first. "Nolan, there's something we have to talk about. Don't shoot Dan Slayter. Just come over with me and listen for once."

"It's some kind of trick," Larson blurted. "Shoot Slayter and listen to her afterward."

Sally ran in front of Dan. "I want you to listen to what I have to say first, Nolan. I want you to hear me."

"Don't endanger your life," Dan told Sally. "Steadman might not shoot, but Larson certainly will."

Dan was right. Larson was going to his horse for his rifle. Steadman, though, yelled after him to stop and turned the Sharps toward him.

"When will you get it through your head who gives the orders here?" Steadman asked Larson.

Larson was standing beside his horse, his hand on the stock of his rifle, when there came the sound of an approaching helicopter. Everyone looked to see a big airship filled with men coming over the tops of the trees from behind them. Steadman and his men crouched first, then made a run for their horses, while a loudspeaker coming from the helicopter ordered them to throw down their guns and surrender.

Steadman and his men ignored the order and

subsequent warnings made by the loudspeaker. Rifle fire began spurting from the open doors of the helicopter at Steadman's men, now all on their horses. The horse hunters, riding for cover, returned the fire. Some of them fell to the guns in the helicopter, while others kicked their horses into a run for the cover of the pines.

Steadman dropped the Sharps rifle and quickly grabbed Sally. Suddenly his horse fell in the hail of gunfire coming from the airship. Still holding her tightly, he forced her onto Keith Larson's horse instead, then climbed up behind her and kicked the horse into a run.

Larson screamed a curse, then picked up the Sharps and took cover behind Steadman's fallen horse. He leveled the Sharps on the helicopter as it came at an angle and turned sideways to sit down. The pilot saw the blast from the rifle and tried to raise the ship. But the bullet plunged into the cockpit, tearing clear through the co-pilot's upper back, then out his chest and into the control panel in front of the pilot.

Sally was yelling as Steadman held onto her while he rode. Leslie had her own rifle out and was going to shoot at Steadman, but she lowered the barrel instead, fearful of hitting her sister.

Exhausted from the fight for his life, Dan was working to regain his breath while he caught his horse and climbed on. His idea was to get to one of the fallen horse hunters and get a gun. Some of the SWAT team were thinking of jumping out of the airship. But it was still too high and the pilot was struggling to keep control.

Keith Larson had reloaded the Sharps and shot again at the helicopter. The second shot hit the helicopter in the fuel tank, opening another large hole, and suddenly the whole helicopter was ablaze.

The pilot tried to take the airship up again but the craft faltered. Steadman and his men all cheered as the helicopter veered off at a crazy angle over the canyon and exploded, sending flaming shards of metal and body fragments far down into the rocks.

Dan had not reached any of the fallen horse hunters yet and did not have a gun to aim at Keith Larson as he reloaded the Sharps rifle. He could only yell to Leslie to ride for cover and kick his own horse into a dead run. He knew there was no way he could ever get anywhere nearly out of range before Larson leveled the rifle.

Dan reined the horse suddenly to the left as the Sharps sounded behind him. He heard the large bullet whizz past his back like a huge, angry bee. Then he straightened the horse again and headed for the cover of the trees just ahead. Once among the pines, Larson would not be able to spot him, and then Larson would be the one out in the open.

Dan heard yelling and, from cover, he looked back to see Steadman and his men coming out of the trees on the other side. Larson was reloading the Sharps. Leslie was coming around the edge of the trees to where he was sitting and Dan saw her suddenly look skyward as another helicopter came into view.

It was a smaller helicopter and it came in over

the canyon and hovered. Larson, holding the Sharps, ran to climb on another horse nearby and catch up with Steadman, who was leading the men back into cover. But the helicopter scared the horse and Larson had to drop the Sharps to catch hold of the saddlehorn and keep from falling.

Larson got his balance atop the horse and considered going back for the Sharps. But the horse under him bolted, and Larson held on with both hands as the crazed animal pounded for the cover of trees where the others were waiting.

Steadman met him, holding Sally firmly in front of him on the horse. She had stopped kicking, as he had told her he would shoot her if she fell off. Now they all watched as the helicopter came in to land. Larson was breathing heavily, still excited from downing the first airship.

"Wished I had that Sharps," he said. "I could get that one, too."

"It don't matter now," Steadman said. "There's nobody on that one that came to fight. Those men are all dead. Now we've just got to get the stallion out of here and we're home free."

He turned his horse and everyone followed him through the dense timber. They had a way to go to get back down into the box canyon, but Steadman was confident now.

"What about that sheriff?" Claude Mosely asked. "He's not dead yet and he ain't given up, either."

Steadman turned in the saddle and smiled. "I've got this little lady, here," he answered. "Slayter wouldn't want her to get hurt, not after all she's already been through."

"I wouldn't count on that," Larson said. "He's not apt to think much about how he goes at us now. Not after what you done to him."

"Just worry about that black horse and what we'll need to do to get him down out of here the back way," Steadman said. "If we can keep him in the timber, we'll make it work. Besides, he's lame and he can't run from us now."

"I have a feeling that stallion is a lot like that sheriff," Claude Mosely said. "I have a feeling there ain't nothing that will keep him down."

Steadman grunted. He moved his horse faster through the timber toward the box canyon. He knew Mosely was right, and he knew they didn't have any time to waste.

EIGHTEEN

Dan was coming out of the trees to meet Leslie as the helicopter sat down. Larson was joining Steadman and the others as they reached a distant line of pines, and finally lost themselves in the thick forested slope.

Dan and Leslie rode up to the helicopter as Williams jumped out and ran over to them. Two men in dress clothes, who Dan assumed were from the FBI, followed Williams. Dan got down from his horse to look into their shocked faces.

"My God, what the hell happened here?" Williams asked, looking around. There were a number of bodies on top and the smoke from pieces of burning helicopter was drifting up from the canyon floor.

"Things went bad," Dan said. "There's been a lot of men die up here in the last couple of days."

Williams shook his head, hardly able to believe what had happened. When Dan told him that one of the horse hunters had shot the airship down with two blasts from a Sharps buffalo gun, he thought Dan was joking.

"Nothing short of high-powered weapons could do that," Williams said.

"A Sharps rifle is a high-powered weapon," Dan pointed out. "It's not automatic—in fact, it's the exact opposite—but it shoots a .50-caliber slug, and that can do some damage."

Williams was watching Dan closely, noting his injuries but also the determination that showed through. It was obvious Dan had been through a lot in the past few days. But this sheriff from Montana wasn't complaining.

It was one of the FBI men who spoke. "Maybe we could have stopped all this had we gotten here when we wanted to. But it was hard to get men together on such short notice. And then when we did, we had mechanical problems with one of the helicopters. Jesus, now what do we do?"

Dan watched the men stare for a while longer. Leslie stayed behind on her horse watching over the ridge. Dan knew she was wondering about Sally and what was going to happen to her. Finally, Williams looked at Dan and asked what they should do next.

"Go back down and get more men up here," Dan said. "That's all I know to do."

Williams looked at Dan closely again. "You look like you might need a doctor's attention," he observed.

"Yes, you'll have to come down with us," one of the FBI men said. "We'll take you to a hospital."

Dan shook his head and pointed to Leslie. "I can't do that. Her sister is a captive now. Steadman has her, and I've got to get her away from him."

"We can send more men in to do that," Williams said. "You might be seriously hurt."

"I'm not hurt that bad," Dan said. "Just go back for more men."

Williams finally conceded and boarded the helicopter with the two FBI men. Dan walked over and picked up the Sharps rifle. A number of bullets had fallen out onto the ground, and he pocketed them. Then he climbed onto his horse and tried to tell Leslie they would find Sally and get her away from Steadman.

"Why did you two come riding in like that?" he asked. "What are you doing up here?"

"It was Sally's idea," she replied. "She just had to find Steadman and tell him something. I couldn't get it out of her, though, even though we're sisters, and very close. She said she could stop all this. I don't know how, but I hope she's right."

Dan fought pain as he mounted his horse. Leslie was still looking out into the distance where Steadman had disappeared with his men and Sally. Finally, they turned their horses and left for the box canyon, where Dan was sure Steadman and the others were headed.

Dan was certain he would be very stiff and sore for at least a couple of days. But he wasn't going to let his injuries keep him from stopping Steadman. He looked up into the sky as the helicopter veered off into the distance, gunning through the sky to bring back reinforcements.

When the helicopter was out of sight, his mind went back to wondering about Sally and if she was now in considerable danger. He could see that

Leslie was becoming more concerned.

"What do you suppose it was she intended to tell Steadman?" Dan asked.

Leslie didn't answer at first, leading Dan to believe she had been thinking hard about it and might have an idea, but didn't want to jump to conclusions.

"I just hope whatever it was, Steadman hears her and doesn't kill her, like he has everybody else," she finally said.

Dan rested the Sharps over the pommel of his saddle and wondered if Nolan Steadman really cared at all about Sally, or if he would leave her lying dead somewhere, the way he had left so many others.

Dan knew they had to act fast now and not depend on anyone else to assist in getting Sally away from Steadman. It wouldn't be wise to try to take Steadman and all of his men at once, not by himself. But there was no question Sally had to be delivered from Steadman's hands.

Sally was inside the small cabin down in the box canyon. The day was ending and there was a lot of discussion among the horse hunters about whether or not they should try to move the mustangs out in the dark. Steadman had been worried about the stallion's leg, but they had checked the horse over and the black was walking and loping without limping noticeably.

But the concern was that if they pushed the stallion too hard, the leg might not be ready and he would turn up lame right out in the open.

For that reason, Larson argued that they should take the herd out right away, in the dark, so that there would be no need to hurry. Others, including Mosely, argued that the canyon trails were treacherous enough as it was during daylight hours. To travel at night was just asking for a fall down into the rocks.

After more discussion, they all agreed that they should wait until dawn to begin their run with the horses. Sally had been listening to it all and had wanted to say they weren't going to make it out, no matter how well they planned it. The odds were against them now, and they should face that.

The men were all edgy, knowing that Dan Slayter was likely nearby and that they would be fighting their way past him to get the stallion out of the canyon and through the mountains. But Steadman was even more determined now than ever, as his armwound was bothering him and he wanted to get it cared for as soon as possible.

Though Steadman had tried to hide it, Sally could see that he was glad she had come back up. He didn't understand just why yet, and Sally had not told him. So far, there had been no chance to talk to him alone. But at the first opportunity, she was going to tell him what she had known now since the day Dan Slayter had come up into the canyon country.

After deciding that they would move out just before first light, Larson and Mosely and the others went out to the herd to watch the stallion and keep an eye out for Dan Slayter, or anyone else who might be coming up after them. Steadman paced the inside of the cabin while Sally watched him. She felt the time was right.

"You wanted to know what brought me up here again," Sally said to him. "Are you ready to listen to me?"

"What is it you've got to say?" Steadman asked. "I've got things to do."

"I'm pregnant, Nolan," she suddenly said. "Did you hear that? I said, I'm pregnant."

Steadman stared at her momentarily and then grunted. "What do you want me to do about it?" he asked.

"Don't you care? Doesn't that mean anything to you?"

Steadman had by now turned away. Sally tried to get him to face her, but he wouldn't.

"I told you I don't care," Steadman said. "Can't you understand?"

"Listen, I'm carrying your child, and I know you care."

"Why should I care?" Steadman snapped.

"Because you *do* care—because you know you should care," Sally told him. "You're confused in a lot of ways, Nolan. You can kill someone without blinking an eye, and not feel one bit sorry about it. But you've never had someone like me before, who was devoted to you for so long. You just don't know what to think about that."

Steadman couldn't speak for an instant. But he finally came back totally defensive.

"You're just another woman," he said. "I've had a lot of them and they're all the same. You're just like the rest."

"Then I guess I'll just leave and go back down," she said, and started for the door.

"No, you're not goin' anywhere," Steadman said, and grabbed her arm.

Sally twisted away from him. "Why not?" she asked. "If I'm just another woman, why not let me go? I'll be out of your life forever and you can find another woman. Isn't that what you just said?"

"I can't let you go now," Steadman said. "Slayter would see where you came from."

Sally laughed. "Don't give me that. Dan Slayter was already in this canyon once. What makes you think he can't find it again?"

"I'm just not letting you go," Steadman said. "That's all. And it doesn't have anything to do with you being pregnant."

"Say what you want," Sally told him. "I know better."

Steadman began to pace the floor again. His breathing was rapid and he looked at Sally often. She watched him and she could see his emotions rising.

"I know you better than you know yourself, Nolan," she told him. "Despite all the lies and all that about being a rodeo queen, you really didn't want to hurt me. I know that."

"None of that matters," Steadman said. He was looking out the window, watching his men as they checked over the horses.

"Yes, it does matter," Sally said. "Right now you want to be happy about the baby, but you don't know how to be happy. You want to say you're glad I'm having your child, but you won't. You can't.''

Steadman finally turned around to face her. ''Listen, I've got to get that stallion out of this canyon. That's all I care about right now.''

''Why don't you stop and think about that?'' Sally asked him. ''Do you really think you can get away with all of this? You're not living in the real world if you don't think Dan Slayter will hunt you until he gets you.''

''I'll get rid of Slayter,'' Steadman said.

''You already had your chance,'' Sally said. ''He's not going to give you another one. Besides, Larson killed a lot of men by shooting that helicopter down with that big rifle. There's going to be more men come up in another helicopter, and they won't stop until they've either captured or killed every one of you.''

''We've come this far,'' Steadman told her. ''We'll make it.''

''No, you won't,'' Sally insisted. ''Use your head, Nolan. This whole thing is crazy.''

Steadman paced the floor and grumbled. Sally watched him, knowing that what she was telling him he already knew, but just didn't want to face.

''Just give yourself up,'' Sally finally said. ''Just tell Dan Slayter that—''

''Are you crazy?'' Steadman suddenly said as he turned on her. ''What would I want to do a fool thing like that for?''

Sally tried to explain the circumstances to him. ''You would go to prison, sure, but with a good lawyer you wouldn't die. You might even get out in time on parole.''

Steadman laughed. "Parole? I'll never go to jail. I just won't do it. I'll die before that happens."

"Then that's what will happen," Sally said, making it sound like a promise. "If that's the way you want it, then go right ahead."

"We've got it all planned out," Steadman said. "We've had this planned for a long time."

Sally could see that he wasn't thinking rationally. He was intent on doing something that might have worked at one time, but could under no circumstances come to pass at this time. Sally tried to explain that to him.

"Nolan, your plans were made a long time ago, before you killed Chuck Farley. Maybe your plan would have worked beautifully if everything hadn't happened the way it did. But now you're a wanted man and that makes all the difference. You can't possibly get anywhere with that stallion now. They'll be watching and waiting all the time. Do you want to be a fugitive for the rest of your life?

"I can see you're going to be stubborn and you don't care about what happens to me or your child," Sally said. "Well, if that's the way you really want it to be, then I guess I can't change your mind."

Steadman looked at her. He could see tears forming in her eyes. She turned away as they spilled down her cheeks. He looked out the window again and at the wild stallion, which was pacing back and forth along the far wall of the canyon, crazed but helpless in the rock canyon prison.

"I can't give up," Steadman said. "I've never

given up in my life and I won't start now."

Sally didn't answer. She watched Steadman move away from the window and join his men outside. She went to the door and watched him, mingling and talking with his men. They were all gathered around and they were intent on what he was saying. They didn't see, as Sally did, the slight movement of two riders who crossed a point of rocks high above the canyon floor.

Sally knew immediately that Leslie and Dan Slayter were up there and they were planning something. She knew now that she had to get away from Nolan Steadman, or become caught in the middle of the showdown that was certain to occur, just as soon as the sun rose in the sky again.

NINETEEN

As darkness fell over the mountains, Dan and Leslie made camp at the top of the box canyon, where the steep sides walled in the bottom. There was a ring of stones there and a number of logs pulled up where men in numbers had camped before.

Dan's guess was that Steadman's men had used the site to overlook the country around them for horses. That way they could figure out the best way to go after them and drive them into the box canyon.

The cabin was just below the campsite, and the stallion and his herd milled about in the confines behind the pole fence. A half-moon rose and bathed the mountains in white. Shadows were deep in the canyons, though, and the trails everywhere were that much more treacherous when the sun was gone.

There seemed little doubt now that Steadman wouldn't try to take the stallion and the herd out until morning. Dan and Leslie had been watching the cabin and the box canyon below for a long time, and there had been no signs of Steadman and the others saddling up for the drive out of the lower end of the canyon. Come first light, there was little doubt Steadman would have his men moving the mustangs.

It had been obvious earlier that Steadman and the others were nervous and eager to get the horses out of the canyon. Leslie had remarked at the time about all the activity. Men seemed to be checking the condition of the stallion continually, watching his movements and noting the improving condition of his leg. There was a certainty among everyone, including Dan and Leslie, that the big black was able and eager to run again.

Besides the concern with the stallion, Dan and Leslie had noted Steadman's constant preparation of details for the run out at first light. He had had all the men pile their gear in one place, so that everyone would be ready to go in an instant. The organization seemed to be near-perfect.

But Dan wasn't worried as much about Steadman's ability to pay attention to details as he was about Sally's well-being. Leslie had remarked about how often Sally had wandered out of the cabin and had looked around, as if she knew someone was up on the rims above the canyon, waiting for just the right time to make a move against the horse hunters.

Throughout the time they had watched the activity below, Dan had comforted Leslie by stating the fact that outlaws always make mistakes of some kind under pressure, and Steadman was no exception. No matter how well he had planned his mission to get the stallion out of the mountains, something would happen that would go against his best efforts.

Now the cabin was dark and it appeared that everyone had turned in to get an early start. The stallion and the mares were even settled down and all was quiet but the howling of distant coyotes. Dan was sitting under a tree, watching Leslie as she chewed on dried meat and fruit he had packed with him.

"You don't seem to be as worried about Sally as you were earlier," Dan said. "Do you think she's content down there?"

"I don't think she's content," Leslie answered. "But she's old enough to know what she's doing. Besides, I have an idea now why she came all the way back up here to talk to Steadman. I think she's carrying his child."

"Do you think that will make Steadman change his mind about what his future plans are?" Dan asked. He had been thinking about it himself for some time and had come to the same conclusion. There wasn't much else that would make a woman do an about-face with a man who had nearly killed her parents. But the question was whether or not Steadman would care.

Dan's conclusion was that Sally would be hoping she could get Steadman to stop all the madness and give himself up. Maybe she hoped he would find in prison that crime wasn't the best road to take in life. Sally would likely be thinking she could change Steadman once he realized he was going to be a father. Now Dan wondered if she had made any headway, or if she had decided nothing was going to change Nolan Steadman.

Dan was watching Leslie now. She finished the small meal and looked out across the canyon.

"Do you think being a father will faze Nolan Steadman at all?" Dan asked her.

"I think he's been a father before and he doesn't give a damn," Leslie said. "But Sally seems to think Steadman considers her special. Maybe she's right. I don't know."

"Let's hope he does," Dan said. "It could make getting her back that much easier."

"What if she doesn't want to leave him?" Leslie wondered, her voice showing that the concern was returning again. "You don't think he'd kill her just because she's carrrying his child, do you?"

"Anything's possible with Steadman," Dan said. "I don't want to cause you a lot of concern and grief, but you asked me and I had to answer truthfully."

"On the other hand, maybe he does love her," Leslie suggested. "Maybe he would want to marry her and raise a family." Then she thought about it. She knew it was merely wishful thinking.

"Maybe Steadman has that in him," Dan said, as if reading her thoughts. "But do you actually think he can alter his way of life now?"

"No, not a chance," Leslie said quickly. "Even if he thought he wanted to, he's got the killer's instinct and he could never quit his ways."

"I'm afraid you're right," Dan said. "Sally can't win either way with him. He's too far gone."

Leslie began to get more jittery, wondering

what lay ahead for her sister. "So, how are we going to get Sally out of there?" she finally asked.

"Come first light, we're going to have to do what we can to try to hold Steadman and his men in this canyon," Dan answered. "If we let them out, we'll have little or no chance of stopping them. We'll just have to watch them ride off and hope that Sally is in no danger."

"What about more lawmen who are supposed to come up?" Leslie asked. "Shouldn't they be here to help?"

Dan was looking out over the canyon, shaking his head slowly back and forth. "By now the news is out that one of Steadman's men shot down the helicopter," he said. "It's probably all over the news. That will make it harder than hell to justify bringing more men up here, unless they're specially trained. It takes time to find men like that, and it takes money. There'll be a lot of political crap over it and finally, they'll send somebody. But who knows how late in the day they'll arrive."

"So you're saying it might be just us by ourselves?" Leslie asked.

"I certainly hope not," Dan told her. "But we can't know at this time."

Leslie was getting more nervous. "How do you intend to stop them?"

Dan patted the Sharps rifle. "This thing shoots a long way."

"And if they decided to use Sally as a hostage?"

"Steadman might think he could use her," Dan said. "But it won't do him any good. Hostages are

207

a method of escape. They can't all escape using Sally. And if they killed her, they wouldn't have a reason to try to negotiate."

"It just seems to me that Steadman will do anything," Leslie finally said. "I don't like it at all."

"Try to get some sleep," Dan told her. "Come first light, we'll do what we can as fast as we can."

"I hope daylight comes soon," Leslie said. "Because I'm not going to be able to get much rest."

It was nearly daybreak and Keith Larson tossed and turned in his bedroll. He was concerned about a lot of things, not the least of which was Dan Slayter and the lawmen who would surely be after them in full force now.

Claude Mosely had been listening to his radio again and they had all heard that the downed helicopter had sparked a lot of anger within the law community. It had been reported that special search and destroy teams were going to be deployed to do whatever it took to comb the mountains and bring the band of last-century outlaws to justice—dead or alive.

This meant their effort to take the stallion out was going to have to go without a hitch. And one major hitch he saw was the presence of Sally Wilkens.

Larson was angry over the situation regarding Steadman's decision to take her along with them while they drove the herd out. She would only slow them down and keep Steadman's mind off the important goal of getting the stallion out of the mountains and avoiding the law.

There had been an intense argument late the evening before between him and Steadman about whether or not Sally should be with them, or if they should just tie her up and leave her behind. At one point Larson had suggested they kill her, thus getting rid of one sure witness against them. Steadman had bristled at the comment and had told Larson there would be no more talk about Sally. She was going with them and that was that.

Now Larson was feeling the urge to take matters into his own hands. Steadman had botched everything up to that point: he hadn't killed Slayter when he had had the chance twice. And now he was going to make it very hard on everyone by showing that he wanted that woman, despite what everyone else thought was best for the group as a whole.

It wouldn't be long until dawn broke—just an hour or less—and then they would have to move fast. He got up from his bedroll and started over to where Sally Wilkens was sleeping. Ordinarily she slept with Steadman, but Steadman had told him he had had some argument with her about whether or not he should give himself up. He had laughed at her and now she didn't want anything to do with him.

In fact, Larson remembered her saying she would get away from him any way she could. And that was why he was up now. If she was serious about wanting to get away from Steadman, Sally

Wilkens would go along with the plan he had in mind.

He made his way softly over to her bedroll and shook her awake. When she started to yell, he covered her mouth.

"I want to help you," Larson told her in a whisper, "not hurt you." When he was sure she understood what he had told her, he released his grip on her face.

"What could you possibly do for me?" Sally asked.

"Help you escape. I'll get you a horse and you can get out of here. Ain't that what you want?"

Sally nodded, hardly able to believe that Larson was doing this. She looked over to where Steadman was sleeping and carefully got up from her bedroll. The other men were sleeping soundly as well, tired from the long days of fighting and running. But there were two guards out at the gate and once she had sneaked out of the cabin with Larson, she asked him how they were going to get by them.

"I'll take care of that," Larson told her. He pointed over to where the saddles and other tack were piled. "Get your horse ready to ride. You haven't got a lot of time to waste."

"What if Steadman finds out you helped me?" Sally asked.

"Yeah, what if I find out?" came a voice from the doorway.

Sally and Larson both jumped and turned to see Steadman walking through the shadows toward them. Sally could see he was holding his pistol, and she heard him cock it. He leveled it on Keith Larson. Then he turned back to Sally.

"Were you goin' to run off with Larson, were you?" he asked.

Sally shook her head. "You know better than that. But I've decided I don't want to be with you anymore, no matter what we discussed before."

Steadman stared at Sally for a time and finally turned back to Larson. "I never could trust you," he said. "Never could."

"Now just a minute," Larson said quickly. "I caught her tryin' to get away. That's what happened."

"Sure it is," Steadman said. "Sure, that's how it was."

Larson started to back away with little steps.

"Stand still," Steadman ordered.

By now most of the men had awakened and were coming out to see what was going on. Steadman told them all to stay back, that he was having trouble with Larson again.

"You ain't havin' no trouble with me, Nolan," Larson whined. He was breathing in short gasps.

"I've told you so many times that I run this outfit, not you," Steadman hissed at Larson. "But you never learn, do you? I don't think you could ever learn that."

"Just wait," Claude Mosely said from behind. "Get this settled *after* we get the stallion out of here. We're goin' to have to work together, and we're goin' to need every man we've got."

Steadman kept the gun leveled on Larson and craned his neck to look at Mosely. "I caught him out here with Sally. Now, I don't know what they were doin'—plannin' to run off together or what—but I can't trust him now, can I?"

Mosely shrugged. "It's just that we don't have time for this."

Steadman turned back to Larson, still talking to Mosely. "No, and I ain't got no more time for him, either. Time to say goodnight."

Steadman pulled the trigger and the bullet doubled Larson over. He gagged and tried to breathe as he fell to the ground, holding his middle. Sally turned away as Steadman leaned over and shot Larson in the side of the head at point-blank range.

"Had to put him out of his misery," Steadman told Sally and the others, and laughed. "I should've done that a long time ago." He turned to the men. "We might as well get moving. We've got to be saddled and ready to go come first light, and that ain't far from now."

TWENTY

Dan and Leslie both jerked awake at the sound of the gunshot. Leslie was immediately on her feet and hurrying to the canyon rim to look over. Dan joined her and they lay prone, straining their eyes in the shadows to see what had happened.

They could see men bending over something near the cabin. Dan knew it was a body. But there was no way to know who had been shot. Then they all left the body and went to their horses.

Leslie pointed to where Sally was being forced by Steadman to saddle her horse. She breathed a sigh of relief. She was alive for now; but if Steadman got angry with her, she would likely die as quickly as anyone else.

Light was now breaking over the canyon. Dan moved quickly to saddle his horse and get to a vantage point over the bottom. Leslie got her horse ready and quickly joined him.

Below, Steadman and his men were quickly preparing for the drive out of the canyon. As Dan got into position, he told Leslie that he felt certain Steadman was not going to try to hold Sally as a hostage. That would cost Steadman and his men time—something they couldn't afford to lose.

"How are we going to do this?" Leslie wanted to know. "How can we stop all of them?"

"I don't know for sure yet," Dan said. "But just be ready to ride. This will all happen at once."

Leslie held her breath as she watched Dan level the rifle. Two of Steadman's men were opening the gate to let the stallion and the herd out. These riders were obviously assigned to ride at the front of the herd with the stallion and direct them.

As soon as the gate was open, the riders were on their horses. The stallion started in a run for the gate and Dan leveled the Sharps on the lead rider.

The gun boomed and the rider fell under the hooves of the oncoming herd. The second rider took off to stay with the stallion and the mustangs, but Dan dropped him from the saddle as well, leaving the stallion to run free.

Steadman saw what had happened and could only tell his men to take cover as Dan opened up on them as well. The horse hunters who tried to get by Dan's aim failed, and soon they were all back in the cabin, or nestled behind rocks.

"Let's catch up with the stallion now," Dan told Leslie. "We have to head him down the canyon toward the wild horse range. We'll have a good headstart on Steadman; let's take advantage of it."

Dan and Leslie rode as fast as their horses would go and came in just ahead of the stallion as he led his herd out of the box canyon. The stallion spotted them and turned the mustangs along the main canyon trail, directly toward where it came out adjacent to the wild horse range.

Dan knew they had to run behind the horses now and get them back to the preserve before Steadman and his men could catch them. There was no other way but to hope they could outrun Steadman; in the narrow passage of the canyon, it would be foolish to try to make a stand.

Dan let Leslie ride ahead of him, while he stopped periodically to turn and watch behind him. Dan realized Steadman was certainly after the stallion, but was no doubt driven more by his desire to settle the feud between them in blood.

The canyon thundered with the pounding of hooves and small rocks and debris flew with the dust that mushroomed into the dawn sky. Dan knew Steadman would have little trouble seeing where they were and by now would be planning how to come after them.

What bothered Dan most was the fact that Steadman knew the country so well and likely had in mind a shortcut that would take him and his men to a point in front of them, where they could cut off the herd. But there was no trail leading up out of the canyon and Dan knew they would have to take their chances going down through the canyon.

The ride for both Dan and Leslie was a nightmare of lurching and bouncing over rocky ground and small ravines that had been cut by wind and water across the time-worn trails. The mustangs were used to the rugged terrain and the stallion led his mares at a dead run, surging through the canyon with a determination to remain free.

As the canyon wound down toward the wild horse range, the trail became more narrow and treacherous. A trail cut off from the main one toward the top of the canyon and Dan wished he could somehow turn the stallion. But there was no hope of that, and the big black horse went right by the trail.

The stallion surged ahead and climbed up onto the trail that led along the steepest part of the canyon. His mares fell in single-file behind him, grunting and squealing as they fought to keep up the pace and their balance along the rocky edge of the canyon.

The trail wound its way along a massive wall of jagged rock that stood straight up from the canyon floor, which became increasingly steep, the rock face stretching farther down toward the bottom with each section of the trail. Dan stayed behind Leslie and yelled for her not to look down. There would be enough trouble staying in the saddle here, without the worry of seeing the distance drop off into nothing just beyond the stirrups.

Dan looked back and saw that a number of the horse hunters were closing in on them. Curiously, Steadman was not among them, nor were nearly half of the men who had started the chase.

Dan knew instinctively that his worst suspicions had been confirmed: Steadman knew the country like the back of his hand, had taken part of the men and ridden along the trail just a short way back. Now Steadman was coming along the top to cut them off where this trail came out.

Meanwhile, Claude Mosely was leading the rest of the men, hoping to box Leslie and him between them.

Dan realized they were trapped. There was little they could do now but continue on and hope to fight their way past Steadman where the trail came out of the canyon.

Mosely and the men with him were closing the gap rapidly now. They could make much better time, as there were not nearly so many horses negotiating the narrow trail. It would be only a matter of minutes now until Larson and the others would begin shooting at them.

The trail just ahead took the herd around a curve in the canyon wall. And just beyond the curve was a deep washout that cut right through the trail. The stallion never broke stride, however, and jumped the washout clean.

The mares followed behind, each one stretching to full stride to get across the deep cut. Most of the herd was now across and when the last three mares reached the washout, one of them hesitated.

The other two horses stopped as well, and when the mare in the lead tried to jump, she didn't make it, and fell into the deep canyon. Dan and Leslie were riding their own horses as fast as they could and Leslie yelled, scaring the two mares into jumping, both making it in turn.

But her own horse made a crazy sideways lunge that threw her off balance. The horse made the jump, but Leslie fell from the saddle and clawed at the steep face of the cliff for her life.

She slid, screaming, as Dan's horse jumped over

her. He reined to a stop and watched as Leslie slid even farther down before finally catching herself by grabbing the trunk of a scrub pine tree.

Dan jumped down from his horse and took both his rifle and a rope from the saddle. His body ached from the beating of the day before as he tied his horse to a shrub. But he knew if there was any time in his life when he would have to ignore pain, this was it.

He watched as Leslie's mare pounded along the trail ahead of them, reins flying, trying to catch up to the herd. He took a rope from his saddle and hurried to the edge. Behind them, Mosely and the horse hunters with him were rounding the curve in the trail. They would be at the washout in less than a minute.

Dan tied the rope around his saddle and lowered one end to Leslie, whose grip was slipping from the trunk of the tree.

"Take that and hold onto it!" Dan yelled down to her. "I'll pull you up."

Leslie struggled to hang onto the tree with one hand and grab the dangling rope with the other. Her strength was fading, as the wind had been knocked from her lungs in the fall. But with Dan's constant yelling and encouragement, she finally managed to grab the rope.

Dan worked with the trained horse, having the animal back up, thus pulling Leslie up the face of the cliff. She was halfway to the trail just as bullets began to ring off the rocks around them.

Dan looked up to see Mosely and the others closing in on them, shooting offhanded from their saddles as they rode around the last part of the curve in the trail.

"Hold on!" Dan yelled down to Leslie, releasing the rope. "I've got to stop them."

Dan leveled the Sharps just as Claude Mosely and the others came onto the straightaway toward them. Mosely was standing up in the stirrups, aiming his own rifle at Dan, just as Dan fired.

The bullet slammed squarely into Mosely's chest, driving him backward off his horse like a rag doll, and beneath the hooves of the horse just behind.

It started a chain reaction, causing the second horse and rider to pile over Mosely's body and tumble off the trail. Three other riders suffered similar fates with their horses, as none of them could stop in time to keep from crashing into one another to avoid Mosely's dead body.

There were three remaining riders and two of them fell to the Sharps. The third toppled from his horse and grabbed for anything he could take hold of before finally slipping off the edge of the trail to fall, screaming, into the depths of rock below.

Dan returned to the rope and worked with the horse once again to get Leslie pulled up over the edge. Once she was in his arms, she collapsed.

"We can't stop now," Dan told her, shaking her. "Steadman is at the top of the trail waiting for the stallion."

After splashing water from his canteen into Leslie's face, she finally revived enough to drink some and get on the horse behind Dan. They would be slowed up considerably riding double, but there was no alternative.

Dan rode as hard as he safely could, urging his horse ahead along the steep and dangerous trail. The herd was not far ahead and he noticed that the stallion had slowed. The reason was plain: Steadman and the rest of the horse hunters were riding along the top, getting into position to catch the stallion as he came up off the trail.

Dan and Leslie both heard the sound of the helicopter at the same time, and Leslie pointed as it came at an angle across the canyon, headed for Steadman and his men. Steadman and the others began to fire at the helicopter, but a burst of machine-gun fire from the chopper sent them into a mad scramble for cover.

The stallion, frightened by the sudden noise of the chopper and the gunfire, bolted forward in a dead run. The big black ran, crazed, for the top of the canyon.

More gunfire erupted from the helicopter and simultaneously from Steadman and his men on the ground. In the melee, Steadman's horse reared and threw him off the side, sending Steadman tumbling down over the bank.

Steadman scrambled to gain his footing, his eyes wide. He was sliding, faster and faster, toward the depths of the canyon. In desperation, he clawed at the rock walls, tearing his fingernails loose, but slowing himself enough to catch his balance on the trail where the stallion was leading his herd.

He was just coming to his feet when the stallion pounded around the last turn before seeing the top. Steadman had no place to go and the stallion was not about to stop.

Steadman yelled and fell backward as the stallion's hooves trampled him into the grooved rock of the trail. He bounced and turned and eventually rolled from the trail and off into the depths of the canyon, screaming and flailing his arms as he slammed against the face of the cliff and then down into the boulders at the bottom.

Dan and Leslie followed the wild mustangs up onto the top and watched as the stallion led the herd along the trail that led from the canyon across an open meadow. Not far ahead was the wild horse range, and freedom for the stallion and his herd.

Leslie was still shaking as Dan helped her down and held her for a time. The helicopter had been circling, dropping men off to surround the last remnants of Steadman's horse hunters. Finally, it landed in the meadow some distance from Dan and Leslie.

Williams was one of the passengers, along with Sally. She had managed to escape Steadman in the chase and they had stopped to pick her up. She jumped out of the helicopter and ran over to Dan and Leslie. The two sisters embraced, glad to see each other alive.

"You two had quite a ride through that canyon," Williams said to Dan. "We picked up Sally trying to ride along the top and catch up to all of you."

"You got here just when we needed you," Dan told Williams. "And I have to thank you."

"No, I have to thank you," Williams said. "Without your help, I doubt if we would ever have gotten Steadman. Where is Claude Mosely and the rest of Steadman's men?"

Dan pointed down through the canyon to the bottom, where the creek flowed and the maze of small canyons broke into the larger one.

"Somewhere down there," Dan said. "I don't know how long it will take to find them."

Williams nodded. He was looking around to where the SWAT team was bringing in men from different directions. Soon the last of the horse hunters were all lying down on their stomachs, with their hands behind their heads.

Williams turned back to Dan. "We've about put an end to this."

"How about Gus and Sadie Wilkens?" Dan asked. "Did anybody think to look in on them?"

"I don't know about that," Williams said. "We just came straight up here. I don't think anybody has looked in on the old couple."

Leslie and Sally were standing nearby now and heard what Williams said. They looked at each other and hurried to their horses.

"I'll go with them," Dan said.

Williams nodded. "I hope nothing has happened to them. You can radio me. I'll see you down below."

Dan had to kick his horse into a gallop to catch up to the two sisters. As they worked their way down the trails from the higher country toward the big canyon that opened up behind the ranch, Dan watched as the helicopter flew over them, filled with men. They would have to make two or three runs to get the remainder of the horse hunters and the SWAT team members.

But Dan wasn't worried about that anymore. Steadman was gone and the stallion was safe. As they reached the ranch house, Dan noticed Gus and Sadie suddenly hurrying out onto the porch. Leslie and Sally broke from behind Dan and kicked their horses into a dead run the rest of the way across the open flat.

Dan watched from a distance while the two girls embraced their parents and laughed and cried and told stories of what had happened. They all turned to him and he tipped his hat. Leslie yelled for him to come down off the ridge to the house, but Dan had already turned his horse and was started for the trail that led down the canyon.

SADDLE UP FOR ADVENTURE
WITH G. CLIFTON WISLER'S
TEXAS BRAZOS!
A SAGA AS BIG AND BOLD AS TEXAS ITSELF,
FROM THE NUMBER-ONE PUBLISHER
OF WESTERN EXCITEMENT

#1: TEXAS BRAZOS (1969, $3.95)
In the Spring of 1870, Charlie Justiss and his family follow their dreams into an untamed and glorious new land — battling the worst of man and nature to forge the raw beginnings of what is destined to become the largest cattle operation in West Texas.

#2: FORTUNE BEND (2069, $3.95)
The epic adventure continues! Progress comes to the raw West Texas outpost of Palo Pinto, threatening the Justiss family's blossoming cattle empire. But Charlie Justiss is willing to fight to the death to defend his dreams in the wide open terrain of America's frontier!

#3: PALO PINTO (2164, $3.95)
The small Texas town of Palo Pinto has grown by leaps and bounds since the Justiss family first settled there a decade earlier. For beautiful women like Emiline Justiss, the advent of civilization promises fancy new houses and proper courting. But for strong men like Bret Pruett, it means new laws to be upheld — with a shotgun if necessary!

#4: CADDO CREEK
During the worst drought in memory, a bitter range war erupts between the farmers and cattlemen of Palo Pinto for the Brazos River's dwindling water supply. Peace must come again to the territory, or everything the settlers had fought and died for would be lost forever!